Praise for *Short Stories Withou*

C000104637

Surrealistic mental nut-punches, with a hea
strong-arming magical realism into crying "
this collection is a mental melange that is be
sitting back and letting it happen (in the best way possible). Tasty
snacks and teasing tidbits that soon have you wondering how you
got here, and leave you wanting more. Buckle up, buttercup--it's a
bumpy ride. And those are the best kind.

USA Today Bestselling Author Tymber Dalton

In *Short Stories Without Provocation*, Yrik-Max Valentonis serves up
a delightfully wide assortment of short tales inserting magic and
fantastical creatures into historical, biblical and everyday settings.
These delightful mini-fables deftly point us to the intersection of
where the Fey connects with our world and beyond.

R.W. Marcus, Author of the *Tales of the Annigan Cycle* Series

Yrik-Max Valentonis has original ideas and an original approach
that combine to create a memorable cross-genre collection.

Richard Lee Byers, author of *The Prisoner Of Tartarus*

Gnashing Teeth Publishing 242 East Main Street Norman AR 71960
GrashingTeethPublishing.com

Printed in the United States of America

ISBN 979-8-9898345-3-2

Library of Congress Control Number: 2024931104

Fiction, Fiction – Short Stories, Fiction – Collected Works

Gnashing Teeth Publishing First Edition

Short Stories Without Provocation
by
Yrik-Max Valentonis

Dedication

This book is dedicated to my dear friend and mentor, Michelle Sauvaget Juristo "Mimi" (1934 – 2024). And for all my friends, may we tell tales, play games, make music, and enjoy the times! For my family, as always; my wife Michelle, son Alexander, daughter Joelle, grandkids Adrianna and Arek. And for all the cats who have adopted me over the years, currently Onion, Avocado, Marmalade, and Licorice.

Table of Contents

-I-
Fables & Follies

THE SELECTED WRITINGS OF IGNOSCIRE THE ETRUSCAN

Selected and translated by Marcus J. Morris, R.W.
for Anselm Hollo and Andrew Schelling

INTRODUCTION

T here has almost always been an interest in the curious customs, manners, religions, and life of the Etruscan peoples of Northern Italy. These speculations begin with the speculations of the Greek historian, Herodotus. Herodotus claimed that they migrated from Lydia and many other early historians like Livy and Polybius, agreed with him. Others, as Dionysius of Halicarnassus, thought the Etruscan people were indigenous to Italy. We still do not have evidence one way or the other on this matter. Unfortunately, there is no surviving record of Etruscan history available.

In fact, there is very little Etruscan writing at all in existence. Most of that is burial script and three books (not intact) on religion: Libri Haruspicini, Libri Fulgurales, and Libri Rituales, collectively called Etrusca Disciplina.

The Etruscan language is unlike that of any other language and is often classified apart from other Indo-European languages. Its translations are still in the speculatory stages. Somewhat fortuitous for us, one Etruscan wrote in what would be called Latin. This Etruscan is Iggy, or Marcus Varibrunuch Ignoscire.

Much more is known of Iggy's life than that of many of his contemporaries. In fact, many of his contemporaries were only known by what they had to say about Iggy. However, most of what his contemporaries had to say was bad. Iggy was viewed as a boring, long-winded, ignorant lout, with exceedingly bad taste, and a horrid sense of humor.

Not much of Iggy's writing survived the passing centuries.
But much comment on him did.

Approximately 351 B.C., a meager student of Plato, Alcman (not to
be confused with Alcman, the Greek lyric poet, 7th. Century), was
transcribing the "Dialogues with Iggy", and wrote

> I have burnt the parchments that contained the
> dialogues between Plato and the buffoon Iggy.
> None will ever have to put up with such drivel
> again. If only I could burn the tenacious Iggy as
> well. I fear that Plato's bad health is due to
> Iggy's unstopping monologue on poppycock,
> which has lasted over a year in length. If this
> Iggy person does not soon leave poor Plato will
> be bored to death.

After Iggy had left (been thrown out of) the Lyceum, 330 B.C.,
Aristotle posted this message:

> If ever you show your face at the Lyceum again,
> I will thrash you until whatever occupies the
> space where your mind should be oozes
> between my fingers.

In 329 B.C., Alexander the Great became so infuriated by Iggy's
harassment of Aristotle and his school that he issued a death
warrant on Iggy. Only a fragment remains.

> ...and if ever found in any region of the Empire...
> right to eradicate... slowly... drawn and
> quartered... vivisected to find... send pieces to....

In 300 B.C., the Museum sent a letter to Iggy, who was currently in
Egypt:

We have heard of your reputation from many
sources. We wish to inform you that if you even
think of appearing at our center, we will hunt
you down like a jackal and stomp you so hard
your Great-Great-Grandmother will feel it.

Iggy took passage on a ship called "Poseidon's Toy", captained by
Virgilius Octave, in 278 B.C.   This is a fragment from the ship's
log

I cannot stand the babble any longer. Three of
my crew had thrown themselves into the water
to escape. There is talk of mutiny. I will crash
my ship on the rocks tonight in hopes of killing
this long-winded plague. If not, maybe I will at
least drown.

Iggy survived, but he mentions that over half of his writing did not.
Iggy became ill due to this incident, and never fully recovered.

Gaius Petronius Arbiter in 62 A.D., wrote of Iggy:

I thought there were miserable people in my
society, until I read about Iggy.
I thought contemporary Rhetoric was trivial,
until I read Iggy.

In 1412 A.D. Pope John XXIII, Pope Gregory XII, and Pope Benedict
XIII, who were all fighting for the true authority of being Pope of
the Holy Roman Catholic Church Empire agreed on one subject:
Iggy.

Pope John XXIII (Balthazar Cossa) "Decree to the World."

... and also the inflammatory and heretical
writings of M. V. Ignoscire shall be burnt....

Pope Gregory XII (Ange Conrario) "Proclamation on Letters."

> ... the Etruscan writer Iggy shall from this day
> forward be considered sinful matter, and the
> reading of such shall be unpardonable....

Pope Benedict XIII (Pierre de Lune) "Damnable Matter."

> ... the worst offense in letters is and always was
> and always will be Marcus Varibrunuch
> Ignoscire....

These decrees were never overturned by any other Pope.

These are other peoples' ideas on Iggy. I myself am perversely fascinated by this historic and literary figure.

Here are his works, for you to judge on their merits and failures.

Sincerely,

Josephine Lake, PhD Anthropology & Archaeology
1993, Katmandu, Nepal

CHRONOLOGY

396 B.C.	Rome defeats Etruscan city of Veii
394 B.C.	Marcus Varibrunuch Ignoscire born in Cortona
376 B.C.	Iggy is sent from home
352 B.C.	Iggy visits Plato's Academy
350 B.C.	Plato dies in Athens
334 B.C.	Aristotle founds the Lyceum
330 B.C.	Iggy visits the Lyceum. Three days later Iggy is thrown out of the Lyceum

| 329 B.C. | Alexander the Great issues a death warrant on Iggy |
| 300 B.C. | The Museum is built in Alexandria. Iggy is sent notice not to appear there |

TRANSLATOR'S PREFACE

The writings of the Etruscan writer and scholar Iggy (Marcus Varibrunuch Ignoscire 394? B.C. — 277? B.C.) have gone untranslated and overlooked by almost all classical scholars. I felt it was my duty to translate this prolific writer, so that the modern world could better appreciate the classical texts that exist.
Current theory is that no Etruscan writing survived the ages. Even though Iggy wrote in Latin, his work disproves the theory, by giving a very different classical outlook on the world which for now, we should consider Etruscan, until proved otherwise.
The normal Etruscan language has not yet been satisfactorily systematized for translation yet, but I and many of my colleagues are attempting to rectify that.

Even though the Latin of Iggy's age did not have what we would view as punctuation, I have included the punctuation marks in his text. I have done this because Iggy's Latin was so poor, or Etruscanized, that it would be almost untranslatable without the punctuation. I have attempted to get to his literal meanings over any poesy he might have attempted to include. These attempts at poesy caused more ambiguity than necessary and obfuscated his already hidden meanings.

I hope I have correctly portrayed Marcus Varibrunuch Ignoscire, his writings, and their impact upon the ancient world of literature and scholarship.

Marcus J. Morris, Translator
Boulder, Colorado, 1993.

Ex Vigilia
Sleep — a wasteful activity that keeps greatness from experiencing the entirety of life. To sleep requires a person to stop talking; to stop talking is to stop interacting with the world; to stop interacting with the world is to accept death; to accept death is to be as a religious philosopher — which is moronic.
A person should always voice all matters of their minds — at all times, to all other people.
...
Travelling is good, so that a person may get an opportunity to talk at more people.
...
The act of sleeping lessens the ability to be aware and flow forth with words which is what language is for — to flow and grow and move on and never rest — as people should follow, like words — endlessly and continuously, never sleeping, never stopping — and always going somewhere else to have more words.
...
Sleep is the evil of the body which must be overcome.
...
... so, a person is sharp, and more understandable without sleep.

Liber Ex Scriptor
The author is free change, thrown at the listener. The listener controls the author during a reading.
...
A reader owns the author, so that at will, the reader may grab the author and control the knowledge that is there. The author no longer is in control. As with the listener — the reader may walk away or stop paying attention. The power of the words depends on the audience.
...
Do the words cost the reader the same as they cost the author to write them?
...
The ideas in literature are always free. These ideas have always existed.

...

Ideas always come with a price. The price of time, the time it takes to think and project order upon them.

...

...only the order and sequence make authors..."

Præter Circa Cognaverint
The study of the past is always a lie of the present.

...

A person who thinks that they know of the past, is a false believer in other's lies about how wonderful they are. The Historian becomes nothing more than a rumormonger for some dead person's vanity.

...

To study the past is to want to sleep without words.

...

The truth of the past is that it never happened- as soon as a word is finished, it no longer exists and therefore must be created again; to try to use a word that does not exist any longer is to lose all words that come after it — hence the past is wordless and should never be spoken of to me again.

...

In my studies of ancient cultures, I have discovered great truths and ideas that mean much for today. Those who have existed before us are what we have become and whose footsteps we will follow.

SINBAD'S ACCOUNT OF THE ISLAND OF WOOD PEOPLE AND FIRE

My crew and I had finally caught up with the caravan of Paridokht the Sorceress at the edge of the Siddim Valley. We had been chasing her for two days, ever since she had captured Prince Nuy'an and fled the great city of Sardis. My crew had been enjoying the luxuries of a stay at home with their husbands after many months at sea. I had been on my way to the palace when I saw a giant, horned, beast-man called the Diwe swarming the walls fighting the palace guards. I rushed to the Apadana. The columns of the large hall were bloodied from attack; the visitors to the court who survived had all fled. I barely avoided being trampled by a giant blue ox being ridden by Pridokht the Sorceress – and there tied up on its back was my Prince Nuy'an. Shortly after we had first met, he had been trapped in an underwater prison by the sea-spawn Atlantians in their attempt to subjugate the coast; I vowed after that to always keep him safe and not let anyone ever take him from me again.

Paridokht and her Diwe fled through the city gates of Sardis. I quickly went through town gathering my crew and we began our pursuit. The sorceress had gained quite a lead ahead of us, but my crew knew how to travel quickly over both the land and seas. We quickly caught up with Pridokht whereupon fifty of her Diwe set upon my women with ferocious rage. Their claws and horns tore into my stalwart companions, who raised swords, spears, and shields to fight back. I drew my nine-foot-long scimitar and cut down a dozen Diwe in one stroke. I leapt across the valley to reach the beautiful and helpless Prince.

I started to untie Prince Nuy'an when the slinky Paridokht appeared next to me. I knew of her from reputation: she was a powerful sorceress from the South, who longed for political control, and had a strong hatred of men. I expected her to instantly attack me but instead, she opened her arms in a peaceful manner and began talking.

She spoke to me about sisterhood and male oppression. She said that as independent women, we were just like each other; we could live in a world without men; we could take power away from men and rule. She said that I was obligated to help out all other women who were being dominated by men. I rebutted her, saying that women and men were equal and that my duties and ambitions were to protect my loved ones. She screamed at me in a jealous fury of her desires for power, control, and love. I laughed and told her that I would crush her and her plans of conquest.

She swore at me, a quite unladylike action, and then attacked me with a magical bolt. The eerie energy pulsated from her hands and encompassed me like a lightning bolt, smoldering my clothes and skin. The pain was excruciating but I remained conscious. I struck her at the junction of shoulder and neck with my sword in order to cut her down, but my strong Damascus steel blade bounced off her without any effect. She laughed and told me that metals could do her no harm.

Pridokht stepped back and waved her lithe arms in the form of magical summoning. The air between us became hot and active as a Dust Devil was conjured forth. She bade it to kill me most promptly. The Dust Devil batted aside my scimitar and slammed me down. It sucked all the air from my breast as it pummeled me. I raised my legs and kicked it like a donkey to get it off me. The Dust Devil grabbed my legs, spun me about like a dervish and tossed me into the sky.

I flew so high that I could see all the lands and seven seas. I looked to the horizon and beheld the Greek giant holding the edge of the sky. I landed hard against the firm bosom of the Moon, who promptly threw me back down to Earth. I called out an apology to the Night Goddess as I plummeted down. She had held a grudge against me ever since her husband propositioned me for his harem.

I still do not know if it was the proposition or my rejection which has caused her animosity, but at least her sisters, the stars, still treat me kindly.

I used the clouds to direct my fall and aimed for a great pelican that was flying by. I landed upon the bird's back and rode her for several hours. We saw no land at that time, so I nuzzled in for the ride. She saw the islands before I did and turned in that direction. I thought for sure she would go to the land, but a school of massive swordfish had caught her attention. She dove down into the sea before I could tighten my grip upon her back. I was jarred loose in the water.

The pelican caught a swordfish as big as a boat and flew off with her supper. I was in the middle of a hundred swordfish darting about attempting to impale any intruder, specifically the pelican who had taken their compatriot. I took a gulp of air, dove down beneath the fencing fishes and grabbed one by the tail. I quickly pulled it down and then thrust it forward, jabbing and parrying the other beasts until I chased them off. I put the nose of the swordfish into my scimitar sheath, wrapped its body around my waist, tucked its tail into my sash, and I swam to shore.

The beach was a field of pearls, opals, and scattered diamonds. It was edged by a thick jungle blossoming a rainbow of flowers, some larger than my head. I kept a watch for anything that might be hiding in the jungle foliage. I walked along the shoreline eastward knowing that in that direction lay my home and dear adorable Prince who still needed me to rescue him.

I came across a small cove and there upon the rocks was a mermaid. She was a smooth, curvaceous woman with breasts the size of cantaloupes and starting at her round hips, she had the tail of a fish. She lay, lounging at the water's edge, her back slightly arched and her naked breasts protruding up to the sun. She saw me and beckoned me closer. I approached and she revealed talons and a mouthful of needle-like teeth with which she tried to ensnare me.

A shark-man sprang from the water where he had discreetly watched. He was gray with the head and fins of a shark but the firm, muscular build of a man of labor (the Atlanteans by difference were greenish in complexion and although quite strong, their physique was very lithe.) He charged forward as the mermaid dove into the water and shot away with such force and fury that a tidal wave was created in her wake. The wave washed over us, stripping the swordfish from me and sending us all flying into the jungle's embrace.

The shark-man picked up my swordfish and proceeded down a jungle path. I gave quick pursuit. The shark-man passed by a great many kinds of beautiful flowers and succulent fruit, past enormous snakes and colorful birds, until he reached a village on the other side of the island.

A group of huts were built circled around a large fire pit, which is where the shark-man stopped. He held up my swordfish in the air and made some noise that I shall generously assume was speech in a foreign language. I saw that wooden creatures surrounded the village. These misshapen wooden homunculi had huge faces with fearsome mouths full of massive gnashing teeth. I assumed these sculptures were representations of the spirits which protected the villagers.

Tiny naked, brown-skinned people poured out of the huts and surrounding jungle. They were just taller than my belt in height. Much like the tribe of pygmies in Africa whom I had visited in a previous tale, these people were not disproportionate but rather just diminutive in size. The tiny villagers surrounded me and the shark-man. There was much strange talking between them and the shark-man. They took the swordfish from the shark-man and brought it to the fire pit and prepared to cook it. They returned the nose of the swordfish to me and I replaced it in my scabbard.

The shark-man crossed the village to the shoreline and walked between catamarans. He tensed all of his bulging muscles taut and dove into the ocean. I watched his powerful strokes as he swam away and eventually dove under the water. I missed my Prince and longed for him dearly as the shark-man's form disappeared from sight.

The villagers escorted me to a pavilion where I was given water, juices, and strange fruits. The fish finished cooking by sunset, and we all feasted under the red, orange, and purple glow. As darkness grew, so did the fire and the warmth of the juices. The tiny people brought forth giant drums, horns made from large pink shells, and a row of leviathan bones that they played with mallets. They played a driving, powerful beat, rocking hard and grooving to the sound. Everyone began to dance and twist like dervishes.

Mistress Moon was at her full glory in the night sky, singing along with their rhythmic procession. She almost didn't seem to mind my presence. Her radiance shown upon the sea, illuminating the waves and currents, and through her reflection I noticed the disturbance; there under the water was fast movement headed towards the shore. The enjoyable festivities had me relaxed and I thought that maybe the shark-man friend of the village was returning. Concern set in. Perhaps this was mere instinct: I had already had too many challenges in my life and so knew not to let my guard down and always be ready for the worst. Besides, as I looked around it appeared that no one else had even noticed the disturbance beneath the moonlit waves.

I pointed to the wake in the water and showed some villagers. The music and dancing stopped as we waited for our new arrivals to emerge. A giant crab scuttled onto shore with a mermaid upon its back. The giant crab charged straight for me with pincers napping. The tiny naked people fled for their huts and the mermaid threw coral shards at me. I knew I had to prevent the crab from destroying the fragile village; the tiny wooden structures would not hold up to its attack. I threw a torch at the mermaid and then headed into the jungle. The mermaid bade the giant crab to pursue me. The path led up a hill and when I reached the summit, I saw I was trapped between the spewing lava of an angry volcano and the giant crab.

The mermaid dove at me but, I avoided her strike. I then jumped upon the back of the giant crab and tried to find a way to pierce its armored shell with my dagger. The beast in return wheeled about trying to reach and chop me with its massive pincers. I jumped off and parried the strikes. As we danced, our fight on the edge of the molten rock, the villagers sang to the volcano, which came alive and bowed. The mermaid fled like a seal.

The volcano erupted beneath me. I jumped back onto the giant crab as the solid ground beneath became molten burning lava which shot us to the skirt of the stars. We fell back down and I landed in the deep ocean.

The bottom of the giant crab had been burnt away and it landed in the ocean like a canoe, next to me. I climbed aboard the shell, ate a bit of cooked crabmeat, and began paddling all night, toward my Prince who was still waiting for me to rescue him.

At the mouth of the Red Sea, I saw the sails of my ship. I flagged my crew and reunited with them aboard my vessel; they had continued the pursuit of Paridokht in my absence. Luck has always been one of my greatest assets and the whims of fate have often shown kindness and favor and thus contributed to my surviving such adventures. My crew was quite pleased that there was enough cooked crab for them all to have some. We sailed through the night and spotted the island where Paridokht had her fortification.

We navigated the ship toward the docks but there was a horrible rending sound and the ship abruptly stopped, throwing us all forward. Shoals rose from the sea tearing apart the hull and stranding my ship. We heard screams from below deck; Farah,

Parisa, and I ran down into the hold to lend our aid to those in distress. I had lost four ships already, so my crew and I were much too experienced in rescue and repairs. I saw Vashti close to the bow where the rocks had broken through the hull. Water was pouring in through the opening. Vashti was pulling timbers and dislodging debris from the site. Vashti was a strong lady with three children at home; she had sailed with me for many years working her way to become my third mate. Vashti yelled over to us that Katayoun and Marzieh were trapped. We rushed in to help. I took a deep breath and submerged to my trapped crewmates. I breathed my air into Marzieh's mouth, she squeezed my shoulders, and I returned to the surface. I told the sisters, Ava and Mahtab, how to help bring air to our friends.

When the Atlanteans had trapped me, Prince Nuy'an had breathed for me in this way. He had learned the idea from the underwater diving helmet used by the sponge farmers. In a way, it was our first kiss and in many ways, it saved my life.

I submerged again and reached Katayoun. I gave her my air, but she did not acknowledge me. I tasted the iron bitterness of blood in my mouth. I looked around and saw that a board had pierced young Katayoun's heart. She had only sailed with me for a few voyages, but she fit in with the crew as if she always belonged. Katayoun was smart, quick with numbers; she handled the sails gracefully and could anticipate the weather. She had not yet married but had several eligible suitors. I felt hands around us, lifting us up. Parisa tended to Katayoun. Vashti pulled Marzieh free and tended to her wounds.

Parisa told me that Katayoun was dead.

We wrapped Katayoun in blankets and placed her on the deck. Farah said a prayer from Katayoun's religion and I spoke our farewells.

We swam from the shoals to the island. Many sailors actually don't know how to swim, but I teach all of my crew when they join. There is an old saying, 'don't trust a captain who can swim.' That's because you know they had to learn. In fact, I learned to swim myself after my second ship sank.

I felt something large bump against my leg in the water. I couldn't make out the shape as it went deep and ahead of me. There are many terrors in the dark waters, so many creatures that most people haven't ever heard of, and many even I haven't seen yet. I put the thought of giant tentacle creatures out of my head and swam faster, encouraging my crew to do the same.

We rested briefly on the shore, hidden by a boulder. We ran up to Pridokht's fortification. It was a large building of Ceylonian design, three stories tall with a wraparound porch entered through repeating archway pillar supports. The porch opened into a courtyard, beyond which lay the fortification's central building. We used every shadow in our path to help hide our approach to the main house.

The Diwe sprang out at us. My crew were ready for the attack though, and instantly engaged them in battle. I fought three Diwe off with my dagger but six more replaced the foes I vanquished. More Diwe came from the main house when Paridokht opened the doors. We were overwhelmed. I felt the fear of losing another crewmate.

From behind us I heard the sounds of movement and feet running across tile. I glanced back and saw a school of shark-men running toward us. They rushed to our aid, attacking the Diwe and opening a path to the front door. I recognized the muscular, well-built shark-man from the island.

I charged through the door at Paridokht. Vashti must have had the same idea because she was already fighting with Paridokht when I approached. Pridokht's hands glowed with a black energy and she slammed them into Vashti's chest. A blinding darkness erupted and threw Vashti across the room, into the wall: she slid down and slumped into a pile, horribly still.

I drew the swordfish nose from my scabbard; Pridokht laughed at me and pronounced me a fool for not learning from past experiences. I thrust the sharp spike into her soft and pliable breast, piercing her heart. She screamed in agony and surprise as her life expired.

I rushed to Vashti's side. She slowly opened her eyes. She said she would live, and I believed her.

I searched the house and found my Prince tied up on a bed in one of the back rooms. I untied him and brought him back to the front of the house with me. The battle was over, all the Diwe were defeated and the shark-men were leaving. My shark-man said something to me that I could not understand. He put his hand to his mouth and then waved at me. Then they were gone back into the sea.

Prince Nuy'an told us where Pridokht had docked her ship and how she got past the shoals. We gathered her treasure and sailed home. And that my friend is how I came across this hand-carved wooden statue that I want to sell to you, and why it is worth the price I am asking.

LEGEND OF THE 12 SKULLS

 hat does the captain keep in that box on his desk?"

"Don't ask about that. It is the captain's secret; he tells no one what is in there."

"I've seen it once. Horrible."

"What do you mean, horrible? What could be in such a little box that is so bad?"

"Skulls. Tiny skulls. A handful of them."

"What kind of skulls?"

"Don't listen to him; he is full of superstition and nonsense."

"Human skulls! The size of a halfpenny."

I.

Many years ago, when the captain was just a master's mate on his first ship, they sailed the Pacific in search of Comte de La Perouse's missing ships. The journey was long and they encountered many terrible storms on the way. His captain was strong on discipline for his crew, many say cruel. The conditions had them workdays straight without break. The sea claimed many tired and unlucky sailors before they reached land. When they reached the Solomon Islands, there was no trace of Comte de la Perouse or his ships. His captain ordered a quick resupply then back to sea. The second mate and chief gunner mounted a mutiny. Many of the sailors were weary of the dreadful voyage and not eager to face the storms again. And they harbored no love for the captain who brutalized them and was so callous about the deaths that had already incurred. The battle was fierce but that captain held his command. He had the mutineers flogged then beheaded. He kept the skulls of those mutineers and gave them as a gift to our captain when he was commissioned on his first ship. They are a good luck charm which wards off mutinies.

II.
Many years ago, the captain was on late watch as the ship crossed a ley-line at midnight. The captain heard the bells toll, as each bell sounded, he heard an echo cannon fire. He grabbed his telescope and scanned the seas but saw naught but ocean. He rested warily on the rail and looked down and witnessed a naval battle of tiny vessels. The Fey world and his ship had crossed and there below were two elfin armadas in combat. The ships barraged each other to sinking. Faerie officers went down with their ships. The captain scooped his hand down and retrieved the otherworldly captains. When morning came, the captain had nothing to show but dry leaves and the skulls. The skulls grant the captain the ability to travel to and back from the Faerie realms.

III.
The captain has been travelling the world in search of all the lost cities of legend. He has been to Tir na nog, Avalon, el Dorado, Paititi, Atlantis, Mu, Xanadu, Prester John's city, Shambala, Shangri La, Saguenay, and cities so long lost that we don't even remember their names. When on land he spends his time in libraries finding ancient maps and books which lead him to the secret lost places. He has followed the travels of Captain Barend Fockesz, Baron Munchhausen, and Sir John Mandeville. At every lost city, the captain has found nothing but ruin and the skull of the ruler. He gathers these skulls together and they tell of how and why their great civilizations fell.

IV.
When the captain was searching for Comte de La Perouse, he stopped at an island chain where the natives carved Tiki. The captain was enamored by these heathen icons but did not take any as souvenirs out of respect for the natives. The main carver was so impressed by the respect that our captain had, he gave to him the

skulls of deceased Tiki. This allowed the Tiki to explore the world and granted good luck to our captain ever since.

V.

The captain has been haunted by a Succubus since he was a young man. This demon comes to him on nights of the full moon, when he is on land, and seduces him. In the morning he finds a skull as a reminder of La Petite Mort. This is why our captain stays aboard the ship when we port.

VI.

Years ago, I was with the captain when we heard and saw a terrible explosion in the sky. It was as if a powder room had ignited. We saw falling stars come from the blast. We took longboats to see where the shooting stars had landed. Our captain is always one of curiosity. We found a burnt crater where the embers had landed. And in the basin of this crater, we found melted shards of metal, a strange glass, and these tiny skulls. The captain swore us all to secrecy and stored away the remains. The captain discovered that when light is shown through the glass fragments charts of the stars appear, but these stars do not line up with what we see in the sky. Late at night you will find him looking at the sky trying to match the patterns.

VII.

When the captain was in the West Indies, he was commissioned to hunt the unrepentant pirates Captains Benjamin Hornigold and Henry Jennings. The elder pirates aided the captain in the capture of twelve dastardly pirate captains. Governor Woodes Rogers hung the captured scoundrels and presented their skulls to our captain. The skulls hold the secret locations to where the nefarious pirates buried their treasures, the captain will eventually go and retrieve the treasure for his retirement.

VIII.

The captain had gone ashore at a remote island. The landing party greeted the local tribe. As they were exchanging pleasantries, a neighboring tribe attacked. The attackers indiscriminately fought both the original tribe and the crew. The captain ordered the crew to defend themselves, so with better weapons of hardened steel and flintlocks, they routed the attackers who outnumbered them. The local chieftain was grateful and bade the group to stay for a celebratory potlatch. At the end of the feast, the Chieftain presented the captain the shrunken heads of the enemy. The meat of the feast had been the hearts of the fallen. The captain took leave of the island to never return and keep the skulls as a reminder of his accidental cannibalism.

IX.
The captain came across a beached whale on one voyage. He took to shore to see if the crew could salvage blubber and whale oil. When he examined the leviathan, he found dozens of tiny tridents piercing it. He searched the shore for some explanation to this mystery. Crushed under the behemoth's fin, he discovered a hunting party of merfolk. He gathered their skulls. Their skulls now tell him the secrets of the ocean currents and where to find fish.

X.
When the captain was a young man studying Philology in Vienna, he met a man at a café who claimed to be the famous alchemist Pretorius. They spent many evenings discussing philosophy and science as those at university are wont to do in their free time. Pretorius claimed to have created homunculi using science to duplicate the ancient Hebrew golem of Prague. The captain naturally disbelieved Pretorius' claims. Pretorius became nervous, saying one of his colleagues was jealous of his successes. Pretorius' house burnt down under mysterious circumstances one night and Pretorius disappeared. The captain went to the burnt rumble and found the skulls and took them. The skulls whisper the secrets of creating life.

XI.

The captain was sent to find what happened to the HMS Friday. With his crew he sailed for months with no trace of the lost ship. On Friday the thirteenth, at dusk, they saw a glowing ship headed toward them. The captain ordered evasive maneuvers, but the ghostly ship kept pace with them at every turn. The other ship would have rammed them broadside but instead vanished. On the deck were the skulls of the command crew. The captain communicates to the land of the dead through the skulls.

XII.

All captains have such a box. The klabautermann, the kobolds who care for ships and bring them luck, go to captains they like and entrust them to guard the skulls of their ancestors. If a klabautermann does not like a captain, they hide the skulls. If a captain mistreats or loses the skulls, the klabautermann curses the captain. Never trust a captain without such a box, for it means there is no luck on that ship.

#

"So, this is how my crew spends their time, telling silly ghost stories?"

"Captain? We were just wondering …?"

"It is just a game."

"Were there any truths in these tales?"

"Maybe…"

HOMECOMING

Uriel stood up and looked again. A person was approaching. Uriel put on her/his armor and stretched out her/his wings. The person was quite far away so Uriel had enough time to prepare properly. It would be quite some time by human standards before the person arrived. Time is measured differently for angels than for humans, people count months and years, whereas angels count millennia and eons. Uriel held the flaming sword in front of her/him and radiated all the Power and Glory of an Archangel. The person continued the approach.

Out of the few people who could find the location of the gate, most of them were unable to live through the final journey to reach it. Uriel had not seen a person attempt the journey in several millennia and it had been at least two eons since someone actually arrived at the gate. They all wanted to enter the garden and had spent their entire lifetime looking for the gate, yet none of them had bothered to get the key first from Boamiel. So, even if Uriel had wanted to let them in, which she/he did not, she/he couldn't. Humans had lost that privilege and they had done nothing worthy enough to regain access to Eden. Uriel reflected on those thoughts about wanting to exclude humans and lead to the Light-Bringer's fall from grace. The old prejudices die hard though, thought Uriel. Uriel had no thoughts of rebellion, only to stand her/his guard.

Uriel recognized the person approaching. This was the first times someone had made the journey more than once. Most people died in the shadow of the gate, either too old and weak to attempt to return from whence they came or unwilling to leave its presence. They erected shrines and dwellings by the feet of Uriel, for they could approach no closer to the gate. Uriel stood as an impenetrable barrier which would remain longer than ever they could wait. They buried the dead that they found when they arrived. They attempted supplications to entreat entrance to no avail. Some attempted conversations and familiarity with the immovable Uriel, which occupied time but did not sway her/his duty. Occasionally a person would leave, discouraged by the impenetrable Uriel and imposing gate, and few would survive the journey through the wasted plains. The likelihood that one should make the journey more than once was nigh impossible. The person who approached was unlike most people. Cain walked directly to Uriel.

"Hello Uriel. It's been a long time."

"Greetings Cain. I have not seen you since your punishment. Why have you returned?"

"I have roamed the earth since then. I have seen all I need to of people. The end of the world will come soon and I want to be home when it does."

"There is nothing left of your home here. It has been destroyed and forgotten for a long time."

Cain and Uriel both surveyed the wasted plains which surrounded the garden. A few blackened trunks and deconstructed walls speckled the scorched earth. The towns, fields, herds, and farms that thrived in Cain's youth were long gone.

"You and I still remember it," Cain said. Uriel looked across the desolate waste and then down at Cain.

"I remember everything. There is nothing special about it. There is nothing here," Uriel stated.

Cain looked at the small dwelling created by the earlier pilgrims and smiled.

"This is still home," Cain rebuffed.

Cain told Uriel about the current state of mankind, its wars and violence and technology and sciences and religions and wars. Cain explained how the apocalypse would come soon and why.

"However, it would appear everyone on Earth has been forgiven but us."

"I have done nothing that requires forgiveness," Uriel said.

"Of course not, Uriel. You are serving a purpose, fulfilling your destiny. But then again, I do wonder, if everyone has been forgiven, why am I still alive, and why do you still need to prevent people from returning to Eden?" Cain asked.

"Cain, did you come here just to harass me with your questions?"

"Of course not, Uriel," answered Cain.

"How long do you intend to remain here?" Uriel asked. Uriel rested the flaming sword back in its scabbard. Cain sat down, stretched his arms out and leaned back.

"I am home Uriel. I have all the time in the world," Cain said and smiled.

BOCEPHUS MACSWEENEY, LAMP LIGHTER OF SOUTH BOSTON

T he creature crawls down the basement stairs and pushes the door open. Sunlight enters the unkempt makeshift apartment, illuminating the man sleeping on a cot. Three bells ring out from the church steeple, the man groans and rolls over. The creature quickly hides behind a pile of clothes tossed on the floor. The man rolls out of bed, onto the floor and proceeds to get dressed, while still lying down. He gets up, puts on his tricorm hat, and walks up the stairs, falling once on the way. The creature watches him and follows.

The man leaves the outhouse and walks to the shed, kicking the fallen leaves of New England's autumn. Inside the shed, he inspects the still and the fermenting casks of his latest batch of whiskey. He opens a bottle and pours a cup to drink. The creature grabs the bottle and runs out of the shed. He chases after the creature across the yard, through the line of drying laundry, and back toward the shed. He grabs the gray, dog sized creature by the scruff of the neck; the creature drops the bottle and shoots quills from its back into the man. The man lets go of the creature and drops to his knees in pain. The creature scurries off. The man delicately pulls the quills from his arm and chest. He stares at the quills.

He thinks "These are real enough, maybe I am not imagining things? Or did I just chase a porcupine and think it was a monster?'" He places the quills in his coat pocket for future inspection and contemplation.

He picks up the bottle and returns to the shed. Three samples later, he locks the shed door behind him and goes to the main house.

"Goodman MacSweeney, you are a mess to behold, and a right shame in the eyes of the Lord. Ye haven't shaved in at least two days, yer frock coat is a rumpled mess, and yer pants are dirty like a child's knees. It's a wonder the Master hasn't sent ye back to debtor's prison," The maid admonishes.

"Apparently, Goodwife Cooper, brotherly love even includes the unfortunate. And the hungry," Bocephus slurs.

Goodwife Cooper serves him a bowl of lukewarm clam chowder and a boiled ear of corn, leftovers from the servants' mid-day meal. Bocephus slurps down the chowder.

"Bait soup and hog feed, Goodwife Cooper, we all eat so well in this new world of ours. Have ye ever wondered what porcupine would taste like? Why, if we eat this, why do we not eat porcupine as well?" He leaves the table still eating the corn.

In the backyard, he spots the creature lurking by the shed door; he throws his corncob hitting the creature in the head, the creature runs off.

Bocephus rubs his eyes and mumbles to himself, Damnable, bad batch of whiskey has me seeing trolls. They'll be putting me in the Bedlam soon.

Bocephus goes down to the basement, sits on his cot, lights a pipe, and reads first, Benjamin Franklin's essay *The Morals of Chess* and then after, Hesoid's *Works And Days* in Greek.

At five bells, Bocephus gathers his equipment (six jars of whale oil, two glass cleaning cloths, a tinderbox, a knife, a handful of cigars, and a flask of whiskey) into his shoulder satchel, a five-step ladder on a rope slung over his other shoulder, and the lamp crook.

Starting at the corner lamp in front of his half-brother's house, Bocephus starts to light the lamps in South Boston. He sets the ladder against the lamppost, climbs up, cleans the glass, refills the whale oil, climbs down, and using the lamp crook, lights the lamp.

He slings the ladder over his shoulder and walks down the street to the next lamp. Lamp after lamp he travels the city. So far, he's lucky, there are no broken glass panes to replace, yet.

At six bells Bocephus notices that he is in front of The Dancing Gargoyle Pub.

The bartender smiles when he sees Bocephus approach the bar: "Is your whiskey to be ready soon? Winter will be here, and you need to clear your ledger."

Bocephus smiles back at the bartender. "I do believe it is my strongest batch yet and in two more weeks I will trade you back for this beer."

The bartender points at a table. "Your famous and fancy chess playing friends are here, if you can tolerate their good and treasonous graces."

Bocephus walks up to the table. "Good evening, Gentlemen Lee, Franklin, and Revere. I'll have this seat."

"That is Captain Lee and Doctor Franklin to you, Goodman MacSweeney," sneers Paul.

"That it is, Mister Revere, thank you for reminding us both of our lowly station," Bocephus rebuts. "Set the chess board, Doctor Franklin, I have been reading your essay again. I am prepared for you."

Benjamin chuckles and begins setting the chessboard. "That one little scribble has caused me such chagrin, for now you are the only man in all the colonies who will offer me any sport."

Bocephus slowly extends his hand palm up to group. "That is because you now spend too much of your time with military geniuses, instead of men who actually think for themselves."

The game and drinking and talking ensue.

Bocephus makes his first move. "The common man sees your gambits at politics and revolution as nothing more than another game of chess — something they don't really understand the point of and know they will be the loser thereof."

"Those who are great men need to make great moves to help the common man be able to actually live up to his worth," says Paul.

"The common man already believes he is worthy. *Ad ogni santo vien sua festa*," answers Bocephus.

Captain Henry Lee III leans into the group and points at Bocephus. "If checkmate can be achieved in five moves, then the common man has little notice of the game and continues mopping the floor uninterrupted, and yet when the game lasts all night, many a common man finds that he can also rise to greatness by those around him."

Doctor Benjamin Franklin moves his Bishop and leans back. "Each man has a greatness within him, if only he strives to achieve it or the world forces him there. Otherwise, he is like electricity; untapped, directionless energy."

"A man's mind needs to be forged and sculpted. Those who strive for greatness are the hammer and the troubling time of the world's injustice is the anvil and conflict is the fire," Paul says.

"Training and practicing are the hallmarks of mental improvement, where schooling leaves off, military discipline picks up the task and directs the mind to betterment and the man, therefore to greatness. The ancient Greeks knew this and so those who served were granted citizenship for they understood the great weight of that responsibility," Henry interjects.

"The classic education spends too much time with impractical and outdated trivial details," Paul rebuts.

"*Bella parole non pascon I gatti*. And so too with poetry, arts, and mythologies. We need our education to be based around science, mathematics, and business," Benjamin says.

"*Bella cosa far niente*. So you, good sirs, would throw away thousands of years of education and humanities for mere trade schooling which any good apprenticeship should wholly provide?" Bocephus asks.

"Over-schooling in the humanities does not produce men of strong character and ability, but only men who spend an inordinate amount of time in the elitist pursuit of the examined life instead of actually living it. Mythology only leads to analytical assessments on primitive superstitions," responds Henry.

"I have been thinking about superstitions lately. I have come to the conclusion that men themselves cause these manifestations, not as you would say Doctor; springeth forth from the mind and imparted upon the senses, but rather, actually and wholly manifested in physical form by the collective will of their like beliefs. Example being; there has been a great influx of Norsemen and Swedes to Boston of late and as such, they brought with them a strong belief in trolls. Now, throughout the town, uhm, people … have been … witnessing the appearances of trolls. And described as such, match the supposed superstition: small gray men with enlarged ears, noses, and hands. And they have quills upon their backs. Visual and confirmed evidence of science and superstition meeting," Bocephus rambles.

Henry shakes his head, offering a condescending look at Bocephus. "Leave it to the grandson of a Salem witch to misunderstand the supernatural and always bring it home to European folktales. In my dealings in the wild with the Wampanoag tribes, they have told me about many of their strange beliefs; it seems Europeans are not the only peoples afflicted with the sin and ignorance of superstition. They have a creature as you described and it is called a Pukwudgie. It too is a small man and playful like a leprechaun but, carries with it the souls of the dead like a banshee. And yes, it can be violent like a troll. You, good sir, in your drunken scientific hallucinations it appears, have gone native."

"There is much we can learn from these natives. We all have heard how they taught our forefathers how to cultivate the foods of the New World. We have bought their magnificent crafts of wood and leather and tobacco. Their democratic politics rival that of the ancient Greeks. If they had greater science, I fear we would have been sent back to Europe. Even the little they have is quite amazing. I have heard the natives use smoke patterns to talk from one village to the next. And I have been thinking we could do the same by using lanterns at night, if we established a pattern of flashes to represent words," answers Bocephus.

Captain Lee gestures at the darkness out the window. "And good sir, all this talk of fires and lamps, wouldn't it be to remind you of the duties you are neglecting currently?"

Bocephus moves his Queen to check Benjamin's King and stands up." Captain Henry Lee the Third, I leave you in command of the board, perhaps you can still manage to lose whilst in a winning position. Send my dearest regards to your gracious wife, the divine Matilda. Mister Revere, may you be elevated by your conspirators' stations and a title when next we meet. And you good Doctor, I hope your next book does not lose you as many games as this one has. Until next we meet. It seems I have actual uneducated work to do."

Benjamin captures the Queen with his Rook. "Check and Mate. *Chi la dura la vince*. Fare thee well."

Bocephus gathers up his ladder and crook and curses the thick night-time fog. A figure darts out in front of him, he trips, falls and drops his ladder and crook. The pukwudgie laughs, puts on Bocephus' tricorn and runs down an alley. Bocephus swings at it with his crook, an arch of fire illuminating the alley, just missing the pukwudgie's leg. Bocephus gets up and chases after the creature. He wipes the blood from his face. The creature darts from alley to alley, Bocephus is lost in the maze of brick buildings, fog, and twisting turns. The creature stops at a dead ended alley. Bocephus charges it.

The creature waves its tiny arms — there is a blinding flash of magical light. Bocephus feels the magic burn through his body. He views buildings and streets rush past his vision as the magic burst throws him across town. He jerks to a stop.

Bocephus finds himself transported to the air over Boston Harbor, whereupon he promptly succumbs to gravity and plunges into the cold water. Bocephus thrashes about in the panic of drowning. Disoriented, he is unable to comprehend and avenue to safety. He lets his body go limp, allowing himself a gentle repose of death in the mighty sea. His still body floats to the surface, whereupon he gasps for air. A short-lived sense of relief is taken from him as teeth sink into his ankle and pull him back under the water's surface.

His eyes Involuntarily open from the pain and in the watery depths he sees that a long-necked sea serpent at least his size and a half has locked on to his leg. He reaches down to strangle the beast, but its skin is too slippery to hold. His chest causes him pain from the internal lack of breathing and underwater pressure which is pushing against the painful punctures from the quills and bruises from his fall. He wraps his arms around his chest attempting to lessen the ache. Then he feels the quills still in his coat pocket. His will of survival sparks his calculating mind; he grabs a quill in each hand and stabs as hard as he can into the beast's neck. The sea serpent releases its bite and smacks Bocephus with its tail as it flees.

Bocephus swims to the shore and sits, breathing heavy in exhaustion and pain, on the rocks. He pulls his flask from his satchel and takes a long drink, swishing the whiskey in his mouth. The pukwudgie scampers up behind him and places the tricorn on Bocephus' head. Bocephus turns around.

"What horror will you inflict upon me next psychopomp? Are you here to take my soul or merely torment me? Wilt thou dunk me in Acheron? Or merely kick me in the shins like a spiteful child? Have you nothing to say? What do ye want, denizen of the spirits? … Spirits?" Bocephus asks. He extends the flask. The pukwudgie drinks and hands the flask back.

Bocephus drinks again and offers the flask once more. "Boston is in the dark and I am in no humor to continue my given task; it appeareth that I shall lose this appointment just as I lost all the rest."

The pukwudgie waves its tiny arm and all the lamps in South Boston are magically lit.

I DON'T WANT HELL

J oshua wasn't the nicest person on the planet, not to say he was the worst. If he had been a Christian, he would have believed in Heaven and might have made it there when he died. But then, you and I both know he died of a heart-attack while summoning a daemon. So it goes. Joshua knew he was dead because, well because; I don't know, I'm only a writer; let us ask him.

"It was odd, you know, almost like what I've heard acid was like. I found myself in this room, I guess, and something seemed weird. The walls were breathing and I felt like I was melting. Then, it occurred to me that I was dead. Sort of like when you have the day off, and wake up at noon panicked, and then realize that it's your day off and it's OK. Wait? Who am I talking to? What is going on here?"

Sorry. I'll get back to the story now.

"So," wondered Josh. "I wonder where this post-temporal Nirvana is, that I'm supposed to go to now that I'm life-impaired?"

To give you an idea about Josh, he was the type of person who said "What?" to every question. And he wasn't deaf.

"Hey you!"

"What?"

See what I mean.

Suddenly, without warning, and very unexpectedly, Josh started falling fast. Really fast. The unique blankness of being in a room without walls which were breathing was replaced by the special effects for every low budget science fiction movie ever made in the sixties accompanied by every color pattern used in the nineteen seventies. Josh screamed.

"AAAAAAAAAHHHHH!!!"

I love that. Sorry again.

Josh falls, Josh falls, Josh falls, Josh falls, Josh falls, Josh falls, Josh falls, Josh falls, Josh falls, Josh falls, Josh falls, then he slows down and stops.

There's a hallway of burning bricks in front of Josh now.

"How am I supposed to get through that? Oh, wait, I forgot, I'm dead." Josh walks down the hallway, until he gets to a door, three days later.

"But time doesn't matter now that I'm dead, does it?"

Right in front of Josh was this huge, gigantic, horrific, supra-imposing, Gothic, bad-assed, killer, fucking, thousand-foot-tall door. And there was no doorknob or doorbell.

Actually, there was a doorbell, but it was at the beginning of the hallway. I won't tell him, if you don't.

"Holy shit! I guess I'm here. Wherever the hell here is?" The door opened. A hand reached out and placed a garbage bag down. Josh slid in before the door closed.

Josh found himself in a stro-pink-green-pastel-nasty-boring-aestethically-puking-generic-waiting room, with a desk for a receptionist on the other side of the room, in front of a closed door.

On the desk was the sign
Take a number

The sign.

Receptionist will be back in five minutes

The sign.

Receptionist wanted

Josh walked over to the desk looking for a number to take. The only thing he saw was a cartoon calendar.

**Freudian Hell
Not admitted without ID**

"This looks promising. Not!" Josh waited, Josh waited, Josh waited, Josh waited, Josh waited, Josh waited, Josh waited, Josh waited, Josh waited, Josh waited, Josh waited.

Josh finally, determinedly, boldly, smelly, stood up and walked over to the door and opened it.

"I guess I've got nothing to lose." So, he thought.

Satan turned and looked Josh straight in the eye (even though between the two of them, there were at least fifteen eyes.)

"Alright smart-ass, you're gonna get it." Josh looked confused. What else is new?

"Get what?"

"The whole flaming thing, hot-boy. I'm outta here."

"What?"

There he goes with those 'whats' again.

"Look here devil-type-person-with-an-attitude."

"Satan. The name is, Satan. OK. My friends call me Sam, but the name is Satan."

"Whatever."

"You can't talk to me like that. I'm Satan."

"Fine. Blow a gasket. I don't believe in you, nor do I believe in Hell. So, I've had enough."

"See George over there. Well, he didn't believe in guns, and he was still shot to death."

Josh stood in befuddled amazement, as Sam handed him the Wand of Orcus and its instruction manual.

In Japanese.

Sam grabbed his bags, as he was walking out the door he said "You'd make a damned good existential protagonist, if you were alive. Ha! Ha!"

Yes. It's true, Satan is the type of person who laughs at his own dumb jokes.

"What…"

There he goes again.

"…is an existential protagonist?"

Sorry. I cut him off before he finished.

A protagonist is generally the character who suffers in a story, the main focus of the narrative trauma. Existential conflicts are when the protagonist has to overcome an aspect of the world around them, generally these are two dimensional characters without many redeeming qualities or charm.

"Oh. I get it. I'm in some idiot's story."

He finally figured it out.

"Well, since I'm Lord of HELL, with fantastic, megalomaniacal, awesome powers, I'll just take care of this."

Wait. I didn't give him that much power.

The writer appeared in Hell. Joshua beat him to a pulp.

"My name is Joshua. Only my mother can call me Josh!"

THE NEED FOR DRAGONFLIES

R osie grabs her backpack and bagged lunch, kisses her grandmother and heads down the road toward school. The sweltering heat and humidity of early summer bakes the road and Rosie fans herself as she walks. The school is less than a mile from her house, but as the seasons change, it feels that the distance grows with the year. She leaves the road and goes down the path through the swamp. Derrick meets her on the path and they go down to the riverbank which they follow to their favorite fishing spot. Every break, all the kids head down the well-worn path to their secret spot, where their parents and grandparents also played.

He is a nice and kind boy, he is not dumb but, fishing is more useful to him than school. He has a future: he can work on his Father's boat after school. He helps out on the boat during breaks and after classes. The family does alright for themselves. He is attractive, muscular in a hardworking way. Rosie has known him since early childhood. She likes spending time with him and now she is starting to really like when he pays her extra attention. Sometimes even getting jealous when she sees him with other girls. She was excited when he asked her to skip school and go fishing today.

They catch a few small fish, throwing most of them back. They make a small fire and cook the one keeper and eat their packed lunches – a true summertime feast. They joke about friends and teachers, swap gossip.

Rosie shows Derrick the trick her grandmother taught her. She stands still with her arm outstretched and whispers. A dragonfly lands on her hand. She holds out her other hand and a dragonfly lands there. Dragonflies surround her, taking turns landing on her.

"How did you do that?" Derrick asks in amazement. Rosie smiles at his interest.

The kiss is unexpected. A fish on her line, his arms around her holding her pole, a tug from the fish, they fall back, the fish escapes, the pole drops, they hold each other, their lips touch, and their passion rises.. They lay there kissing and holding each other, passions that are budding adult feelings, years of friendship, and pleasure. They embrace and enjoy the moment for all it is and could be.

Awkward silence. Rosie gets up. They stared at each other. New found desires in their thoughts, fear and uncertainty. Where does this lead? When? Should we continue? Should we pretend this never happened?

"We better get home. School is almost out and we don't want to get caught playing hooky," Rosie says.

"Yeah. We better," Derrick agrees.

Rosie picks up her backpack. They walk back to the road silently holding hands. The beginning. At the road they look at each other, awkward – to kiss again, to just turn away, what to do?

"Do you want to, uhm, go fishing again Friday?" Derrick asks. Rosie smiles, blushes, and nods. Derrick gathers his nerves and briefly kisses Rosie on the lips. They turn and each go home. Rosie's grandmother is waiting for her in the kitchen.

"So, tell me about school today," Grandmother says.

"Well, it was school. Nothing to really say," Rosie answers. She looks down at her shoes, looks around the kitchen, at the gas stove, looks anywhere but at her grandmother.

"I know you weren't at school. I know you spent the day with that Thompson boy," Grandmother says.

"How did you know?" Rosie asks.

"The dragonflies told me. You know if you lie to me they will sew your lips shut. Now be a good girl and tell me everything," Grandmother demands. Rosie tells her everything, everything except the part about the kiss, she is not ready to admit that to herself, let alone her grandmother.

The next morning Rosie timidly gets ready for school and goes to leave.

"Girl, are you so ashamed of yourself that you can't give your grandmother a kiss before you go to school?" Grandmother asks.

"No ma'am," Rosie answers and kisses her grandmother.

"You are a good girl, make sure you remain that way. Stay away from that Thompson boy. Mind your studies and learn a lot, so you can make a good life for yourself. Now go to school," Grandmother says.

Down the road Derrick joins Rosie on her walk. They walk in silence for a bit.

"I got a whupping," says Rosie.

"Me too. I'm sorry," Derrick says.

"It's OK, I know," she says.

They go to school.

After school Derrick goes to the docks to help his father unload the boat and clean up. Rosie talks to her friends and watches Derrick leave. She sees a man in a red suit and shiny black shoes standing in the shade down the road. The after-school gossip concludes and everyone starts their journey home or to after-schoolwork.

The man in red approaches Rosie. She feels a jump of anxiety and before he speaks, she turns and hurries away. He follows. Rosie cuts through McGregor's field the fastest short-cut home. She walks faster and faster. The man in red stays behind her showing no effort in keeping pace. She is sweating but he is not. The cows wander away from the trespassers. The dragonflies take flight as Rosie approaches. Rosie looks over her shoulder to see where the man in red is, but she doesn't see him behind her any longer. She turns back around and he is standing right in front of her.

"Who are you? What do you want?" Rosie screams at him, her fear getting the best of her nerves.

He smiles.

"You know," he says.

"Why?" Rosie asks.

"Rosie, what do you want? I can make sure you get it. Absolutely anything or anyone," He offers. Rosie trembles, she feels the sweat bead up on her forehead and roll down her back. He stands there smiling in his red suit, not a trace of sweat or discomfort from the heat.. She looks at his shiny black shoes still, clean in the middle of the dusty field.

"You can offer me anything? And nothing bad will happen to me if I take your offer?" she asks.

"Yes, you can have anything. Just as I said," he answers.

Rosie looks across the field to where she can see the roof of her house past the trees. There is so much she wants. Her desires parade through her thoughts. She could have a good life, be comfortable, be wealthy, live in the city, have Derrick's love. She whispers to herself.

"You didn't answer my other question," she says.

"Nothing bad," he answers. The dragonflies swarm around his head. They sewed his lips shut. His face contorts in anger. He shakes his fist at her. Rosie smiles. The man in red disappears.

Rosie feels cold and shakes. She runs home.

MIRIAN, A TALE

hris takes the first exit he can find, inching along the highway, face nearly touching the windshield. He pulls under the overpass, turns off the windshield wipers, and parks. *I'm not gonna make it to Atlanta tonight. Can't even see the road through this rain.* He climbs into the back of the van and falls asleep.

At first the story came easy enough.

A troll lived under an overpass to the out-of-town highway. The troll's name was Mirian, but nobody ever called the troll that, because nobody knew the troll. I'll call Mirian, "Mirian" for I made Mirian up and I'm writing a story called "Mirian, a Tale" about a troll named Mirian, who tells stories to bricks which are the patio of a writer (or at least they end up that way), who hears the stories and writes them down.

Mirian walks around the metal box with wheels. It looks like the things that go over the overpass, sometimes they go under the overpass, but this is the first time one has been so close. And not moving.

Mirian tries talking to it, but it doesn't respond. Mirian touches it: it is cold and wet, like a sword in the lake. Mirian climbs on top of the box, and it opens. Out of it comes a people. Mirian watches the people.

Mirian tells me a tale; something I want to believe, something that was always within me. Something self-determined. I begin writing. My characters are becoming a part of my life. They exist. I think something's wrong. Am I writing about people or am I writing up people? Only god can create.

He wakes up at the first crack of dawn, gets out of the van to stretch his legs before he starts driving again. While he's pissing behind the bushes, he notices a pile of bricks under the overpass. *No one's around. They don't seem to belong to anyone. I could finish building my patio with them.* Chris puts them into his van and drives home.

The wind is as strong as when the animals were stolen by people, when it rained. Mirian holds tight. "Hi Meg. It's good to be home. How was your weekend?"

Mirian jumps off the metal box when it enters a box cave. Mirian watches the people as it hugs another people. They touch faces. Mirian sees that the people have bricks too. The people's bricks are behind the box cave, arranged to be a floor. Mirian watches the people make the floor bigger with Mirian's bricks. There is a smaller box cave by the bricks where Mirian sleeps.

"What the Fuck" Mirian looks around for the fuck, only seeing the people drop his goblet. "What is a fuck?" Chris fumbles for a cigarette, drops it, picks it up, drops his lighter, picks it up, sits down and lights it.

"You. Oh. A. You." Pointing his finger at Mirian. "Oh boy. Uhm. You."

"I'm not a fuck. I'm a troll. Mirian, troll. Mirian. Troll."

So, this is why I can call Mirian "Mirian" for I made Mirian up. Of course, if you asked Mirian about this, Mirian would claim that I was made up by Mirian, so there's no point in asking either one of us. Unless you were curious, then I suppose you want to ask one of us, but I'm not sure you could ask either of us, since we're both fictitious characters, or maybe we're real and you're not, or maybe you don't care and just want to hear the story. But you're reading it.

The problem is I think I'm having a nervous breakdown, which I blame on Mirian, or maybe it was the demons. I'm not sure, yet.

Mirian was 3'17" tall, Mirian would have been 4'5", but trolls can't count that high. Mirian would have told people that Mirian was green, but like I said before, Mirian doesn't know anyone to tell, except me, but we already discussed this. Mirian was actually blue, but that wouldn't matter much since trolls are color-blind. Except for being able to see purple, yellow, red, orange, and some color that they call gulibwicz. Sometimes, I wish I could see a color with a name like gulibwicz, but I'm not sure why I would want to, I'd probably be disappointed.

Most trolls don't know people, and only get together with other trolls once every three hundred and seventeen years (by human standards of telling time; how trolls tell time is a story in itself). And of course, when they do get together it becomes quite the party. After all, there's a lot of socializing to do after so much time. Since trolls are alone for a great majority of their lives, they tend to find hobbies to occupy themselves with.

Mirian's hobby was bricks. Mirian loved bricks. Every brick Mirian met was a brick Mirian loved. Mirian realized however that indiscriminately snatching bricks for the brick collection would lead to obsessive behavior patterns and a great pile of obviously absconded bricks, which would lead to Mirian's bricks being repossessed and Mirian in need of personal re-associating. Mirian concluded that selective collecting would enhance the collection of bricks. After all, a troll had to show something impressive to the other trolls (in a friendly, competitive way). So, Mirian only collected the bricks that were the first brick from a brickyard.

Mirian did more than just collect bricks - Mirian also played with bricks. More specifically, built things (there's not much else to do with bricks, even rare ones). Mirian's favorite thing to make was a floor. Mirian would lay all the bricks on the ground so that their edges were touching and they all together generally looked like a large flat brick from a distance. Mirian built other things as well; but when the bricks were arranged like a floor, Mirian would tell them stories. Mirian had lots of stories. More stories than one person could write in two lifetimes, they just kept coming and coming, sometimes (often actually) more stories would start before the others were finished.

Chris heard the tales from Mirian and saw himself in them. Each story was an excerpt of his life, no matter how modified or convoluted. Meg was the analysis and theory to Chris's work and actions. Mirian spun tales which stacked ideas together until an object was constructed.

Meg was the first audience. Chris would bring her the stories he was drafting; sometimes he left her waiting on the finished work. She would ask or demand for completion, satisfaction, a resolution to the story.

The bricks waited. The bricks listened. The bricks were immensely useful, they could be the foundation to build upon or they could be a sounding wall.

Life is how the universe observes and understands itself. Stories are how memories become. People are how trolls avoid boredom. There was a troll who once lived under an overpass.

Mirian invented Chris and his van as a way to get beyond the overpass, for even trolls look to the other side of the bridge.

-II-
Auntie Boneyknees

CHICKEN'S FOOT

T he journey is like a chicken's foot, behind there is the path which you came and in front of you are the three paths which to choose your Baba. And this is just scratching at the surface. Stories are told often and great stories are told more often. Good storytellers give many facts and great storytellers give many details. A story takes a while to tell and sometimes longer, but living the tale is longer still, the story always goes by faster than the act itself. There are changes made in the story's telling to make it more tellable since a story is no longer the life as it happened but now has its own life and it is reborn with each telling.

In the dark woods of the heart of the old country, the three sisters Baba lived. They each lived in a magical izba. They had been there as long as any person in town could remember. They never seemed to age, even though they were each a different age; one young, one middle-aged, and one crone. Many people thought the sisters were the Three Fates of ancient Greek mythology due to this similarity. It is interesting to see how people will reduce such simplified commonalties in an attempt to understand something, instead of actually investigating what they are curious about. The sisters did nothing to hide and the people did nothing to look. The sisters were less fates of people than they were tests for heroes.

The three Baba kept mostly to themselves and remained alone, except for the occasional brave adventurer passing through or a hapless lost soul. All three Baba followed the old customs; their doors were always open and a pot was always warm in the hearth, for although they liked the solitude of forest life, they were hospitable to all wayfarers. As is the case of lonely meandering roads through the forests and auspicious crossroads, many people managed to find themselves there confused, lost and the subsequent stories about the choices they made, so the Baba were not in want of happenstance visitors.

Each izba was alike: a small, square, log cabin with a stove and chimney in the center. Each izba had support   under it, two giant chicken-legs which would occasionally spin the izba around or dance. The izbas had one other magical quality of being larger on the inside than they were on the outside. This last quality came in handy in that the Baba never had to worry about storage space or room for visitors. It really is surprising that the Baba had any visitors at all, since surrounding their izbas were fences made of bones and gates made from ribs and capping off the posts were human skulls, which burned with magical fire.

A flock of black geese land in the yard of Baba Yaga and enter her izba. They tell her of a hero on a quest coming from the Kremlin. Baba must test this hero, to prove that he is worthy, but he is going another way and will not pass her. Baba Yaga walks from her izba to the large pestle in the yard. Baba Yaga hoists her skirt up; she raises an ancient varicosed leg up and places her foot on the edge of the pestle. In one swift step she gets inside, throws a broom out in the yard. The flames in the skulls on the fence recede. All the bones collapse into piles on the ground, they clack and chatter, hop and nudge, there are grinding and snapping sounds as the bones reconnect themselves into thirteen giant skeletons. The flame seeps from the skulls and envelopes the skeletons. Then they stand and fall in line behind Baba Yaga's pestle. The legs beneath the izba stretch out and claw at the ground, they thrust and jerk and stand up. The izba walks in a circle three times and falls in line behind the giant flaming skeletons. Baba Yaga's pestle rises into the air and flies down the path. The skeletons follow the pestle, the izba follows the skeletons, and the broom follows the izba. The broom sweeps away the tracks of the procession.

The flock of black geese flies off to the izba of Baba Jezi. When Baba Jezi and her izba move, the geese go and tell Baba Noga, who also moves her izba.

A man who thinks of himself as a hero, rides toward his first real challenge.

CHILDHOOD GAMES

regory, be home before dark and don't go far into the forest or Baba Yaga will catch you and eat the flesh from your bones," Mother calls out.

"Yes Mother, I'll be home on time." And he means it. Gregory was just as afraid of Baba Yaga as he was afraid of Mother's spanking. It was even worse if Father got upset.

Gregory quickly runs from the cottage to the far side of the cabbage field, where all the village children are already gathering. There is a field past the cabbages with some trees before the forest begins. The path that leads into the forest is wide and well known. The children have some secret paths into the forest which lead to a clearing. The real secret was which adults use those paths at night for rendezvous. He hears Od and Olaf arguing as he runs. Od and Olaf are brothers, almost a year apart. Olaf is just slightly bigger and older than Od.

Gregory stops and picks up a stick. A stick is one of the most wonderful and magical toys for a child, it has an almost limitless potential for transformation and use. Gregory knocks a rock in front of him with the stick. The rock skips four or five feet ahead and Gregory runs in that direction and hits it again. The game with no rules and one player is immensely satisfying and meditative. Walk, walk, hit, and run. Walk, walk, hit and run.

"Stop bickering. We can play a game we all like," says Helene.

"He will only play sissy games. I am a real man," Olaf says.

"You are just a baby! And play stupid games," says Od.

"You are the baby! I'll show you!" Olaf says.

"You can't," says Od.

"Stop it! Stop it! Stop it!" says Helene.

"We will play Cossacks and Gypsies! Od is the Gypsy. Get him!" Gregory speaks.

Gregory swings the stick and hits Od hard on the right thigh. Od yelps and his leg buckles. The other children join in hitting Od with sticks and their hands. The sticks, they pretend, are the whips and swords of the Cossacks. Helene takes two steps back and chews on her lip. Od runs. The chase is on. The other children pretend their sticks are horses and ride after him. Od, not encumbered by the awkward motion of pretending to ride a horse, is able to get to the closest secret path into the woods well before anyone else.

Od sprints as fast as he can through the path. Jumping over protruding roots and downed branches, ducking and swerving he makes it to the clearing. He hears the others behind him, he runs to the next path. He climbs down the riverbank and hops across the rocks in the shallow of the stream. He runs along the bank and climbs up a path that is hardly used. He sees Gregory still behind him. Od ducks behind a boulder and crawls under the shrubs. He follows the hill slope to another clearing. He is crying, hyperventilating, unable to speak, he can barely see with the tears. Gregory is shouting, he is madder than ever before. He does not like this chase anymore. Od should have stayed in the first clearing and taken his beating; it would have been over by now. They could be doing something else, they didn't need to be so deep in the forest, so far from the path. Gregory cannot and will not stop until he has his satisfaction of hitting Od. Od is too scared to stop, Gregory will not stop.

Od crashes through the creaking gate without looking, he bangs on the door whimpering and gasping. Gregory runs at him but stops at the gate. The skull turns toward Gregory, the eye sockets of the skull have fire inside and appear to be staring right back at him. The front door of the tiny wooden cottage opens. Od collapses.

"What is this? Why am I to be disturbed so? Is this how you come to my house?" The voice is harsh and demanding.

"H... h... h... he ... h... h... hur... hur... hurt ... m... m... me." Od stammers the words, barely audible through his crying and wheezing.

The emaciated, ancient woman stands in the doorway, glowering from boy to boy, as if she could see not just through them, but inside them, like she is analyzing the parts that made them. Her back hunched her almost in half, bringing her long, blue nose down close to Od.

"I smell the stick of your fears. Coward's blood." She snarls at Od, her few remaining tusk-like teeth snap with each word.

"P... pl... plu... please..." simpers Od, who upon looking up at the old woman feels an even deeper fear than before.

"No." Gregory exhales.

Gregory steps his foot back and raises his stick, trying to ward off what he is seeing. The skull looks at him. The fence and gate which are made of skeletons reach an arm out and pull him into the yard, depositing him on the doorstep of the izba. He sees the giant chicken legs folded underneath the izba. Baba Yaga turns to Gregory and sniffs.

"You have the stink of a bully," she snaps at Gregory.

She stands there watching them both, thinking, analyzing, smelling. Od cries more.

"It's your fault, coward." Gregory says to Od and hits him with his stick.

Baba Yaga nods her head. She has made her decision. She waves her hand over Od. He feels his chest tighten, he pulls his arms and legs close to his body. The pain runs across his entire body. Like a shoe that is two sizes too small, a full body corset being tightened by the Devil, hammering a square peg into a round hole, Od tries to scream. Gregory is transfixed watching as Od transforms into a mouse. Baba Yaga smiles with her remaining teeth.

"Marinuska! You know what to do with these two." Baba Yaga yells into the izba. A young woman comes out of the izba, scoops up the mouse, grabs Gregory by the ear and brings them into the izba. Marinuska brings Gregory to the kitchen and puts him down by the firewood.

"A bully quickly becomes a coward when bullied. A coward can learn how to become a hero when having to defend someone else. Some tests are passed, and some are failed. You get what you earned in the end," Baba Yaga says.

"Put the wood on the fire," Marinuska commands Gregory. Gregory opens the grate and places several logs in the fire. Marinuska opens the huge oven door and brings a pan to the rack.

"Get on the pan." Gregory looks at her, he looks at the door, feels stupid for leaving his stick outside and he looks at the pan which is big enough to hold a hog, or him. He gets in the pan and lays down. Marinuska slides the pan into the oven. She stands by the oven watching as Gregory is cooked alive. When he is fully cooked, Marinuska slides the pan from the oven and prepares Baba Yaga's meal.

Baba Yaga sits at the table and eats Gregory. Afterward, she carries a bag outside where she climbs into her giant pestle. Using her mortar to fly the pestle and having her broom sweep the tracks behind her; Baba Yaga leaves the bag at the cabbage field.

Helene wakes early; she slept badly, waking frequently thinking she heard Gregory or Od return. After breakfast, she leaves the house to meet the other children, her parents let her go without having done any chores. She is the first to reach the edge of the cabbage field. She sees the bag. She opens the bag and screams.

HOUSEWIFE

hen the faeries sprinkle dew over the leaves and flowers, Baba Jitnaya awakens. She puts on a marigold dyed dress. She spreads out a small white cloth on the table, places a piece of bread in the center of the cloth and anoints the bread with salt, and then she ties the corners of the cloth together. She goes across the dewed yard to the barn. She places the cloth into a worn-out boot hanging on the barn wall.

"Accept this gift and bless my family and our crops."

Baba Jitnaya returns to the kitchen and lovingly boils the porridge. The rooster caws. Even with no chickens left, the rooster still performs his duties, and just when will he be eaten too, she wonders. Her husband and two sons sit for breakfast.

"Porridge again!?! Will we never get any meat in this house?" grumbles the youngest. His brother hits him and scowls. Her husband stoically begins eating his porridge.

"What? I'm sick of porridge. It's all we have had for weeks. And adding a sliver of potato or bread doesn't make it any better." His brother goes to hit him again.

"Stop. That's enough for the two of you. We will get by and be able to have meat again soon. We just have to survive this hard time. Maybe growing corn will be our success. Your Father is willing to try anything to keep this farm. We just have to work hard and believe. Complaining and fighting won't get anything accomplished," admonishes Baba Jitnaya.

They all eat their porridge in silence.

"After this harvest sells, Bogdan, you should ask that sweet girl Jelena to marry you. You would have beautiful grandchildren for me," announces Baba Jitnaya.

"Oh Mother. Please let me get through a meal without you planning my children," retorts Bogdan.

After breakfast, her husband and sons go to tend the crops.

Baba Jitnaya washes the bowls and spoons. "I am sick of porridge too. This crop had better be worth staking our livelihoods on. How much longer can we go on like this," she thinks. She inventories their remaining food, a loaf of bread, three potatoes, a beet and an onion.

She begins her daily household chores; washing, sweeping and cleaning; there are no longer any livestock for her to tend. When she finishes, she begins to mend her family's worn out and torn clothing.

Nikolai, having the youngest eyes and doing the least amount of work, sees the rider first. The rider's armor glints and sparkles across the field as the sun reflects from it.

"Father, do you see? A   man on horseback approaches," Nikolai calls to Gleb.

They go to the path, escaping the claustrophobic corn shoots. The men stand together waiting the rider's approach, enjoying the brief and unexpected break from their labors, not even minding the mid-day heat, now that they have access to a breeze.

Tzarevitch Vasilii watches as the men gather on the path. "Like cows, these peasants, gathering in dumb-struck awe at any shiny item passing by," thinks the possible future Tzar.

"Hello there, people. I am Tzarevitch Vasilii. I rule this land. I need a place to rest and food to eat," he says.

"Our home is just down this path. Be polite to my wife and you will have the food and rest you need," says Gleb.

"You do not tell me to be polite, peasant," thinks the young Tzarevitch as he rides on.

"Sons, we have more work to do and only so much day to do it in," Gleb says, ushering his boys back into the oppressive fields.

Vasilii sees the white cloth sticking out of the boot on the barn. 'These ignorant peasants still have the old superstitions, leaving boots and gifts for domovoi, house spirits. How pathetic,' thinks Tzarevitch Vasilii.

Baba Jitnaya hears the horse and rider approach the house. She goes to the porch to greet her visitor.

"I like the way the sun shines through her dress, as if she's not wearing anything. I guess there is some good to the peasant life," thinks Tzarevitch Vasilii.

"I am Tzarevitch Vasilii, I rule this land. I need food and rest," he says.

"Come in and take off your armor. I will make you some food to eat and will clean your armor as you rest," she offers. "What can I possibly give to a Tzarevitch? I don't have enough for my own family," she wonders. "Maybe he will be generous and leave us some rubles."

Baba Jitnaya prepares a bowl of porridge and boils the potatoes, beet and onion into a soup. She serves that and half a loaf of bread to the Tzarevitch. She finds her tea leaves drying on the counter. 'How many times can I use these tea leaves,' she wonders.

Tzarevitch Vasilii looks at the meal, weak tea, over-cooked porridge, sparse soup, and stale bread. "Maybe being a peasant is worse than I thought. Isn't beet soup supposed to be an aphrodisiac? These silly superstitions they have. Thank goodness at least I am educated," he thinks.

He eats enough to fill himself, more than her entire family eats in a day.

"Give the rest to my horse," he demands. Baba Jitnaya makes sure to hide enough for her family's dinner.

"Do you have any vodka?" asks Tzarevitch Vasilii as he settles onto the couch.

Baba Jitnaya gets the bottle and dusts it off. She pours him a drink and puts the bottle on the table next to him.

She brings his armor into the kitchen and gets down on the floor to clean it.

Tzarevitch Vasilii drinks and watches her. He analyzes her the same way he selects which horse he'll ride in the stable. "She is old enough to be my mother, but then again, my Father has had women younger than me as lovers. There is a touch of grey about her, and wrinkles, and some flab. But on the whole, she is well preserved and shapely," he thinks.

His mind races as she rocks back and forth on her hand and knees scrubbing his armor. He finishes drinking the bottle just before she finishes cleaning his armor. He staggers to his feet and stumbles into the kitchen. She catches him as he falls. He regains his balance and quickly twists her arm.

"Now woman you'll give me the hospitality of your bed," he says, pushing her to the bed.

He grabs the neckline of her dress and pushes her onto the bed. Her threadbare dress tears and shreds down the front leaving her exposed.

"No," she demands. The Tzarevitch laughs and takes off his clothes. Baba Jitnaya closes her eyes and concentrates. She focuses on what her grandmother taught her as a young girl. She opens her eyes and sees him naked and ready.

Baba Jitnaya transforms.

Her right claw tears through his chest leaving his ribs exposed and broken. Her left claw grabs his throat and tears it away, his head flops down onto his chest. He looks her in the eyes. She plucks them out. His body falls to the floor.

Baba Jitnaya mostly transforms back. There is always a price to pay every time this magic is used, a little of the change always remains.

Baba Jitnaya puts on a grass green dress. She uses the scraps of the marigold dress to clean the blood from the floor. She takes the meat to the kitchen and guts and debones it. She puts the bones in a bag which she places at the edge of the corn field. She cooks up and preserves the meat.

Gleb and the boys return after sunset but before the night becomes cold.

"I see that our guest is still among us," announces Gleb as he enters the house.

"No, my dear, he has departed us, but he left us some gifts in his passing: rubles, armor, new clothes, boots, and a horse," answers Baba Jitnaya.

"Mother? Have your teeth grown? And I don't remember your ears being so pointy?" asks Nikolai.

"Boy, your mother is beautiful and precious. Tell her so. Tell her you love her. Let her know how much you appreciate what she does to keep this family together," says Gleb.

"Come let's eat," she says.

They all eat their dinner in silence.

"You know Bogdan, when we sell the armor, you could afford to ask Jelena's parents to let you marry her," announces Baba Jitnaya.

"Please Mother, let it be," pleads Bogdan.

SWAN AND WOLVES

Koshchei the Deathless leaned over his scrying pool. He searched for the closest Baba to attack, for his plans required a preemptive strike to force the Baba to retaliate. He saw the image of a large bird flying nearby. He poured enchanted oil over the wolf pack, casting a spell:

May the anointed be protected-
No sword cut-
No dagger slice-
No axe hack-
No arrow pierce-
This oil makes them armored.

Koshchei dropped a burning ember on the image of the bird in the scrying pool. The wolves howl.

Mikhail looked up at the fireball in the sky and stumbled over a rock buried in the snow. His feet ached from the cold and the stumble twisted his knee. His hunger gnawed at him and his fear of knowing the Tzar's taxman would be waiting for him battered his mind and spirit as much as the weather battered his body. It has been too cold a winter, the forests have been too heavily logged, the animals over hunted, the Tzar keeps sending troops across the country to different wars, and they need supplies and arms and food, but the men who build and farm keep getting conscripted into the Tzar's army and sent away from their homeland and they are not there to farm nor hunt nor build any more, yet the need keeps growing.

Mikhail saw a pack of animals in a clearing ahead. He circled around to use what little covering he could find. When he got close enough, he readied his bow and notched an arrow. He studied his prey – a small pack of wolves attacking a large bird. The wolves were unnaturally jet black and larger than a bear. Their eyes glowed green, and their growls and barks sounded like echoes. The bird was as large as a woman and looked vaguely like a swan - mottled gray and white with light green highlights. The bird appeared to be too injured to fly. The strangest thing about the bird, and maybe this was because it couldn't fly, or it was due to its large size, it had a confidence which he had never seen in a bird before; the bird put all of its energy into fighting back, scratching with its talons, battering with its wings, and pecking with its beak, instead of trying to escape like most birds do when confronted on the ground.

Mikhail aimed into the melee. He had to decide upon a target. The bird was obvious his goal, it could feed him and provide enough meat to give to the Tzar's taxman, it would make this hunt worthwhile, even without bagging anything else, but if he killed the bird now, the wolves would feast upon it and there would be no way to separate them from this kill. He would have to kill at least one of the wolves - there are only five of them, and after one died, he reasoned he could scare the others away. The trick would be to find the pack leader and kill that one first, to demoralize the pack; it would be easier to control the rest once the leader is defeated. Mikhail aimed at the wolf directly in front of the bird, it was the largest and most likely the pack leader. Mikhail let loose his arrow.

The arrow flew straight toward the heart of the beast but the arrow bounced off its hide. The pack now is aware of Mikhail. The pack leader glared at Mikhail. Two wolves break off from the fight and charged Mikhail. As they closed in on him, Mikhail fired arrows to the head, heart, shoulder, gut, and legs of the wolves, each arrow bounced off the wolves' hides. Mikhail drew his sword and dagger as the wolves reached him. His strike landed solid on the back of the wolf and the power of the bounce back nearly knocked the sword from Mikhail's hand. He thrusted his dagger straight into the chest of the wolf and the rebound painfully twisted his wrist, knocking the dagger from his grasp. The wolf pounced on Mikhail, knocking him on to his back. Mikhail hit the wolf in the throat with his sword. The kickback wrenched the sword from Mikhail's hand.

The wolf bit Mikhail's shoulder, its teeth tearing through his quiver strap. Mikhail tried to roll away, but the wolf swatted him down with its claw, the nails ripping his coat to shreds. Mikhail punched the wolf in the nose. The wolf's head rocks back and blood dripped from its nostril. Mikhail continued his attack, kicking the wolf in the ribs and hitting it in the head repeatedly. The wolf on him staggered away from his assault, providing the room the other wolf needed to attack. Mikhail is tackled by the second wolf, bitten, clawed and battered. In desperation, Mikhail grabbed around for anything he could find to force the wolf off him; from his gear, he found his fork, which he thrusted through the underside of the wolf's jaw into its skull. He jerked the fork back and forth with all his strength until the wolf collapses. Just as Mikhail stood up, the other wolf jumped on him, sending him tumbling. He found his broken bow and when the wolf lunged again, he speared the beast in the throat.

Mikhail stood up again. He saw that the bird had managed to kill two other wolves; only the pack leader remained alive and fighting. The wolf crouched, preparing to lunge at the bird, which raised its wings and bellowed a thunderous honk; a lightning bolt hit the wolf, killing it instantly. Mikhail gathered his sword and dagger and approached the bird.

The bird spoke: "Please do not kill me hunter."

A long time ago, Ivan had told Mikhail about all the troubles he had when a fish spoke to him. All the adventures Ivan had to go on, all the dangers he had to overcome, all the monsters which attacked him; Mikhail was not sure he was prepared for such a lifestyle change but perhaps giant speaking birds are not so prone to adventuring as speaking fish. And Mikhail was very tired and hurt from the battle with the wolves, and the bird seemed capable of throwing lightning bolts, which was a compelling enough reason to not try to kill it. Mikhail could not determine how injured the bird was and he did not want the bird to know how injured he was, so he presented a show of strength.

"Why should I not kill and eat you bird?" Mikhail postured. He prepared his sword to strike the bird, making a show of his readiness to fight. But the adrenaline left his body and the pain and exhaustion crept over him with its cold. Darkness clouded the edges of his vision. Mikhail was unable to tell if the bird was answering him or not as he collapsed. The bird spread her wings over Mikhail's body.

Marie contemplated killing the hunter after he collapsed. Her wings covered his entire body, he lay unconscious and vulnerable. She could easily crush the life from him as he lay there. It would not take that much effort. She had enough strength to finish him. His good looks swayed her slightly, he did help her fight off the enchanted wolves, and she was tired; she would not kill him this time. She covered him and she too succumbed to exhaustion. Mikhail fluttered his eyes — pen - blood, sweat, cold, and the weight of the wing had sealed them shut. Aching in every muscle, pain in every joint, stiff in each movement, Mikhail slowly rolled over and pushed himself up, first to his hands and knees, where he caught his breath and then he stood. It had snowed, in the time since they had fallen. He scooped the snow off the bird which had blanketed them in a tent-like igloo.

Mikhail pulled and dragged two wolves next to the bird and tied their legs together. He bound a rope around the wolves and secured the bird in the center and dragged the capture to his home. He noticed that the bird was still breathing. It would be ridiculous to bring a bird into the house, place it in his bed and wrap his blankets around it, truly a foolish thing to do, something a madman who has been alone in the woods too long might do. Mikhail wondered just how crazy he really had become. Was he even home or was he imaging that as well?

When Mikhail was young, he had traveled to France with his parents, there the houses had separate rooms for each activity. A room for living and gathering, a room for cooking, a room for eating, and a room for sleeping; this dividing the rooms of houses left such a strong impression on the young Mikhail, that when he grew up, returned to Rus, and built his own house, he made it with rooms just as he remembered. The outside of the house looked like any other log room house in the area. The rough-hewn planks and large chiseled boulders gave a look of stability to the house. The windows were shut tight against the winter. However inside, the rooms were decorated with French flairs and aristocratic accents. No one had visited Mikhail's house, but they would have been shocked to see a tub in its own room inside — amazed to see fancy legged end tables, which Mikhail carved himself, attempting to duplicate the French scroll work he remembered. They would have been curious about the paintings hanging on the walls, landscapes of French country sides and castles. When he was not hunting or chopping wood, Mikhail spent time with his artistic pursuits and displayed his favorite creations around his home. He was a renaissance man in the deep woods.

When Mikhail went to town to sell furs, meats, and timber, he saw how other people lived. He saw the simple one room houses, where entire families slept in one bed and there were no interior walls. He could not invite anyone to his house, he knew they already told enough stories about his strangeness. He had thought occasionally of bringing the intricately carved furniture and paintings to town to sell, but then questions would be asked and he did not want to become a liar. His crafts made up for his solitary life.

He heated water for a bath. He gathered vodka, scissors, needle and thread. Mikhail bathed. He sewed shut the deepest wounds. The ones he could reach. He alternated pouring vodka on the wounds and drinking it. He dried and put on his night clothes. He filled a basin with warm water and carried it to the nightstand by the bed. Mikhail pulled the blankets halfway off the bird. He moistened the washcloth, cupping his hand under its head; he washed the bill, the head, and neck. He rinsed the cloth in the basin. He poured vodka on the cloth and carefully cleaned the injuries on the head and neck. He rinsed the cloth again.

He washed her shoulders. He disinfected the wound she had on her left shoulder and sewed it shut. He rinsed the cloth and wiped the wings clean. He washed her breasts. He caresses her absentmindedly. He rinsed the cloth. Feathers brushed up and down his arms. He washed across her stomach. She put her arm on his back and slowly rubbed, lingering softly by his wounds. He dabbed vodka on the scratches across her ribs. He removed the blankets off the bird entirely. Feathers caressed his face and across his chest. She sighed. He lowered his head. She slides his nightshirt off him. He shuddered. She rubbed feathers across his stomach. She gracefully changed into the shape of a human woman. She kissed him hard, banging teeth into lips without a care. He grabbed her by the back of her head. His fingers knotted through her hair, pulled her kiss tighter.

She wondered how this magic occurred, was it destined for them to bond? He wanted to never be away from her and he knew she felt the same. How could he know what she felt, but he did. He knew this was primal magic. This, which was not supposed to happen for either of them, had united them forever. They wondered how this would change their lives. Sleep overtook them.

Marie woke and looked around the room noticing the furniture and paintings. He is not like the other peasants she realized; perhaps his differences will make him acceptable to Grandmother. This is not how she was supposed to find a spouse, this was not the man she was supposed to be with, but what is done is done, and he is who she is with now. He had style at least, and bravery enough to fight the wolves… And her. He brought her to his home and cared for her. He put her in his bed and took care of her. That was something. He could have left her, he was injured, he threatened to kill her, but when he had the opportunity, he saved her. He saved her, surely Grandmother would see that as passing the test as proof that he was worthy, a sign that he could be a hero. Some heroics are small gestures, not all heroes save the world and defeat the armies of evil. Sometimes just being a good person and providing for your family was enough to be a real hero. Yes, Grandmother would understand that and accept him.

She rolled over and looked into his hazel eyes. Mikhail had been awake for the last twenty minutes, watching her. He smiled behind his trimmed beard. He tentatively stroked her cheek. She smiled back at him. He moved closer and embraced her. She rested her head on his chest. Even if Grandmother did not accept him, Marie had. They held each other.

"I don't have to be anywhere, but I do need to go hunting. The Tzar's taxman will be coming soon with many soldiers, and if I do not have something for them, it will not be good. My bow broke while fighting the wolves. Now, I must rely on traps. There is some food here to which you can help yourself," Mikhail explained as he dressed.

"I will go with you. You can bring the wolves and give the taxman the meat from them. We will skin them and use the hides," Marie announced.

"A woman can't do this type of work. What are you thinking of, eating wolf meat; that is disgusting," Mikhail protested.

"I am not just any ordinary woman, or have you already forgotten yesterday? And I did not say we would eat the wolf meat. I said we can give it to the taxman," Marie explained.

Mikhail stared at her. He placed his hands on his hips. Marie stared back at him.

"Well, I think I like having you around," Mikhail said.

They brought back the three other wolf carcasses and the few arrows which were not broken.

"I need to clean my weapons and put them away. It is not good for them to be dirty for so long. It will dull the blades. They go in the house, so I will be in the house for a while. Cleaning them," said Mikhail.

Marie watched Mikhail go into the house. He was up to something, she could tell. That was a weak excuse to clean and store his weapons, but it gave her the chance she needed. Marie walked past the shed and smokehouse.

Mikhail checked to see that Marie was not around. Mikhail pulled the bookcase away from the wall, which glided silently on the hidden casters built into the base. He opened the hidden door. In the hidden closet rested his helmet, breastplate, greaves, bracers, and shield from when he was a cavalier in France. His three magic arrows also rested there. Mikhail picked up his helmet, he had once worn this armor in service of the French King. He upheld the ideals of chivalry and the life of a courtier. He fought honorably. But honor gets lost in wars and even worse, never enters politics. The so-called nobility are deceptive, traitorous, and murderous all in the quest of greater wealth. Being a cavalier was to be a pawn in their internal struggles; the honorable knight-errant sent to battle in petty skirmishes over vanities. Mikhail placed the helmet back. I am no one's tool. I can fight back. He placed the magic arrows into his quiver.

Marie walked to the edge of the woods. She stopped and looked around to make sure that Mikhail was not around or watching her. Marie transformed into a swan and took flight. She swooped through the woods, darting between trees as fast as she could go. She soared straight up over the treetops and circled around the woods. She saw movement, a fox. She dropped like a hawk, flying full speed straight down, she caught the fox and transformed back into a woman on the ground.

She held the fox by the neck with her right hand. Marie's hands transformed into sharp claws and her teeth became tusks. She invoked a spell:

> *By this creature's blood –*
> *Through the entrails spilt –*
> *As the forfeiture of life –*
> *Let me see tomorrow' path –*
> *Let me know the correct way to travel –*
> *Give me the future's map.*

She stabbed her claw into the fox, pulled out all of the bones and waved them over her head, then cast them into the pool of blood.

She hunched down, kneeling at the edge of the pool and watched:

> *A bird makes a nest. Fox running circles. Singing drunkard.*
> *A fire rages. An arrow. A sword cuts a tapestry.*
> *Frog milk. A ship sets sail. Bag of gold.*
> *A stag runs. Fish in a purse. A garden in bloom.*
> *Baba's izba dances. A horn trumpeting. Crocodile dancing.*
> *A river of fire. Broom mover. An army surrounds a castle.*
> *A Bear standing upright. A bird makes a nest. An arrow.*

She picked up the fox's skin and waved it in the air. She placed it over the pool of blood and entrails like a rug. She scooped the edges and squeezed the cut back together. When she let go, the fox was no longer cut, she kneaded the fox's body, like a sculptor with clay.

"Have a full belly this week and better sight for the rest of your life," Marie whispered into the fox's ear. The fox shook its head, looked at Marie and quickly ran off into the forest. I should put a protection spell around the house, but I don't have time right now. I need to get back before he begins to suspect something. It can wait until later, Marie thought. Marie transformed into her swan form and flew back to Mikhail's house.

Mikhail came out of the house and walked to the wolf carcasses. Marie joined him. They hung the carcasses up in the smokehouse.

"There is a magic spell on these wolves. It protects them from weapons. We will have to find a different way to skin and cut them," Marie explained.

"My fork worked well enough. Tools seem to be able to penetrate their hides. We can try the shearers first and worst comes to worst, we can use sharpened stones. I have some in the shed," Mikhail said.

"Why would you keep sharpened stones in your shed?" she asked rhetorically.

"Well, I never know when I might need them, like now," he answered. He brought back three sets of shearers, one of wool shearers and two gardening shearers. They bled and skinned the wolves.

"The shearers work well enough. I guess you don't need your sharpened stones anymore...." joked Marie. They tanned the hides.

"We can make coats, hats, and gloves from these."

"Will the protective magic remain on them?" asked Mikhail.

"The magic should stay on them forever. We can test it first. I don't know if the protection will be as strong as it was for the wolves, but it will add some benefit," said Marie.

Mikhail buried the heads, tails, and paws in a compost heap. Mikhail cut the meat; Marie fried the meat with brown sugar. She filled the bottom of the barrel with the cooking grease and placed the cooked meat on it. They salted the hides and hung them to cure. Three days later the taxman arrived. Mikhail and Marie watched as the group of horsemen and a wagon approach.

"You should not be seen by them, I think. It would be best if they had nothing new to think about when they leave here," Mikhail said to Marie.

They kissed and she hid in the bedroom. Marie poured water into the washing bowl and cast a spell over it to act as a scrying pool so she could watch what was going on. The riders came straight to the cabin, three soldiers dismounted, one of which banged on the door. Two of the riders flanked the wagon. Mikhail waited a few moments before he opened the door.

"Who is this visiting my cabin deep in the woods?" asked Mikhail as he opened the door.

"Where is your contribution for the Tzar's army?" asked the taxman sitting on the wagon bench next to the teamster.

Mikhail looked at the three soldiers surrounding him and his door; he looked from horseman to horseman, the teamster, and finally looking the taxman in the face, eye to eye.

"It has been hard finding game; however, I lucked upon a sounder of boar. I potted the meat in a barrel. It is all I have to give. The barrel is in the shed," Mikhail said.

"Go with him," the taxman told the dismounted soldiers. They followed Mikhail to the shed and searched it while there. The lead soldier opened the barrel and inspected the contents, digging into it with his dagger. He had one of the other soldiers taste the meat. When he was satisfied, Mikhail and the soldiers loaded the barrel in the wagon.

"The Tzar is pleased with your loyalty, we will be back next season," the taxman said. Mikhail watched them depart then he reentered his house.
"Their tastes are as refined as their manners" Marie said to him and they laughed.

GRANDMOTHER HATES ME

I think we will visit Grandmother today," says Marie as casually as she possibly can. Mikhail looks at his wife. He can tell she is nervous. He sees the clues: she is absent-mindedly preening the hairs on her arm with her other hand, she does not look at him directly but turns her head sideways to see him from her peripheral vision, and she clucks her tongue on the roof of her mouth. He smiles; she could be an actress pretending to be a swan with her gestures. Marriage removes the acting and pretending, the people let their guards down, the masks which are presented to the rest of the world are removed. With time and patience, the partners get to see the truest form of each other, the primal self: the person who existed before the parents gave them a name. Casual clues and habits develop and are learned, the understanding between them becomes instinctual, on a level usually beyond words but on feeling and intuition.

In the past few months they have been married, he has heard mention of Grandmother from Marie. She has tried to use euphemisms and vague generalizations as much as possible. He had a grandmother of his own. He cannot understand why Marie is so nervous and anxious about her grandmother. Marie has been trying to prepare him for meeting Grandmother, without giving away some secret.

She is like many other Grandmothers.

She is a strong woman with strong convictions.

She had a certain type of man in mind for me to marry.

She is very demanding.

Things must be done in a particular fashion for her.

She might be unhappy.

Her anger has no bounds.

Please keep an open mind.

No matter what, do not offend her or be rude.

Mikhail knows that Marie is afraid that Grandmother will not approve of him, after all not only is he a meager hunter, his parents were Francophiles who spent a great amount of time in Europe. Also, there is that small matter of Marie actually being a giant swan. Or is she a person who turns into a swan? Or is she some type of spirit being both swan and woman? Mikhail has not received a clear answer on that from Marie, but it does lead him to the belief that Grandmother would want for Marie to marry someone who could at least change shape or possess other magic al qualities. Mikhail came back to his homeland and settled down to a simpler lifestyle. There are times when wanderlust strikes him, but all those journeys have made him relish the peaceful stable life he now has. His marriage deepened his desire for a quiet life with a consistent routine. It provides him with security he had missed during childhood. And Ivan, a friend from his past, visits often enough to bring news of the world and adventure to satisfy his fancies of exploration. Ivan has warned him about the world of magick; how important it is to not ask for anything, to realize how easy it is to be tricked and that one should never offend a magickal being for their wrath is strong and long lasting. Ivan knows too well. Mikhail has always kept magick at an arm's distance.

He has been preparing himself to be a polite and courteous in-law for whatever scorned magical bird being he might meet. Since he grew up in France, Mikhail is only vaguely familiar with the Russian myths and folktales. He is not sure what Marie is or what Grandmother could be. He has heard of the Firebird, the Double-headed Eagle, and Dragons. He has heard of Dragons all over Europe, but Marie does not seem to fit that description. He has heard of werewolves, maybe there is something similar with swans, he has pondered. He did not hear many folktales in France, there was a cat that wore clothes and could talk, a prince enchanted to be a wild boar, but no birds that he knew of. And he had been wracking his memory ever since he met her months ago.

Mikhail had wished Ivan would have visited at least once before Marie made this expected but dreaded pronouncement. Ivan had been Mikhail's only real friend and they had been friends since Mikhail had returned to Russia in his early twenties. Ivan grew up in Russia and new Russian folklore, but more specifically, Ivan had once met a talking fish. This encounter had put Ivan into an adventurous journey and by all reasoning gave him an understanding of the mythical world that most people just did not understand. Ivan did not frequently visit Mikhail during the winter, not that visits to Mikhail were common occurrences due to how deep in the forest he lived; but during winter, the journey was harder and there was less food to share, so Mikhail was not surprised by his friend's absence. Mikhail had just hoped that in the occasional unexpected turns of Ivan's life one would bring him to visit. But no, this time it was Mikhail's life which had become an unexpected journey into the mythical realms.

"Should I bring something? Some meat? Wine? Vodka?" asks Mikhail.

"No. Grandmother wouldn't want anything like that. Mikhail, there is much I haven't told you yet. Things that are important. It matters to us. It explains who I am and who I need you to be. I am not sure how to tell all of this to you. There is a war going on," says Marie.

"I know that much. The Tzar has his armies attacking all of the Nine Kingdoms. That is why the land has been so ravaged. The soldiers were all killed   off or scattered too thin and now all the farmers and woodsmen have been conscripted to be soldiers. The soldiers still need food and supplies so the remaining people have to work harder to provide for the soldiers and because the soldiers used to do that work, there is now more work for less people. The supplies and food don't stay with the people, but instead are sent away with the soldiers. That is why I have had such a hard time hunting and trapping. That is why we cooked magical wolves for the taxman, to provide for the soldiers. The soldiers are good people; it is the Tzar who has decided on this, not them," says Mikhail.

"Yes, there is the Tzar's war, but I also mean that my people are in a war, too," says Marie.

"The birds. Uhm … Bird People? Uhm? Shape Shifters?" questions Mikhail.

"Well, I haven't really explained that to you. And I can see you have thought about it, but still have not quite grasped it all. I will try to explain. I am a magickal person. The magickal beings are also at war. The undying wizard Koshchei has been planning something big. I am sure that he is the one who hit me with a fireball and sent the enchanted wolves upon me. He has an affinity for both striking at a safe distance and wolves. It felt like his magick. We know he is planning to attack us and that seemed very much like an exploratory attack. It will come very soon. The warrior-king Byely Polynin has been battling Baba Yaga for as long as I can remember and before that too. He also has found something new to use in his war against us and is building his strategy on how best to implement his new powers. King Bear has sealed the borders to his kingdom. No one knows what he is up to or whose side he might be on. We speculate that he is increasing his magick and his armies, but we cannot know to what strength or purpose they will be. There are others as well, some small factions around and many individuals who have yet to choose a side and may never truly be on anyone's side but their own. I am a part of a sisterhood of magickal beings. There are three levels in the sisterhood: Sister, Aunt, and Grandmother. Baba Noga is my grandmother in the sisterhood. We are closer than family. For us, family was not always a good or pleasant thing, but the sisterhood is. We have obligations though, duties to perform. Marrying the correct person at the correct time is one of our duties, it is one of the ways we fight this war. In marrying you, it might have been seen that I have forsaken my obligations, even though I know marrying you was the right thing for me to do, so don't ever worry about that. It is just that we must now find out what Baba Noga thinks about all of this."

"So, I am now a part of all of this magickal world and warfare?" asks Mikhail. No longer will Ivan be the only one with tales of the magickal world," Mikhailo thought. He was now the one with a new tale to share and many more to come.

"If Baba Noga accepts you ..." Marie whispers.

"What happens if she doesn't?" asks Mikhail. Maybe he won't be around long enough to share his tales, which is one of the drawbacks and dangers of adventures. The great possibility of mortal harm helped shape his decision to lead a quiet life. Battling magickal beings is never a pleasant proposition, but being a pawn in a magickal war is not much better. Marie was right, finding the correct person to marry is very important.

"Well, I want you to know I love you," he says.

"I love you too. We should go now," says Marie. "I will fly us there; you may ride on my back." Marie transforms into a giant swan. This is how Mikhail had first seen her, when Koshchei's wolves were attacking her. Mikhail notices that she is bigger now than she was then. She did not have a passenger then, he thinks, that is why she was not this big, for if she was this large, those wolves would have not been able to put up quite the fight they did. Mikhail stares at her for a minute, thinking, she is quite the swan, graceful, elegant, and beautiful even when she is a person, but at this size, she could feed the entire village for a week and there she is unsuspecting right next to me. Well, that is the hunter thinking not the husband.

"Is anything wrong? What are you thinking about?" asks Marie.

"Oh, nothing dear," answers Mikhail and he climbs onto her back. She spreads her wings and takes to flight. They lift into the air. Mikhail has a vivid memory of climbing trees as a child, how one of his friends said that he could live in the trees forever. Mikhail had not thought about climbing trees in a long time, he enjoyed the wave of nostalgia, he enjoyed the feeling of freedom that the height provided him, the freedom of self-sufficiency that climbing gave him. Mikhail knew these memories were because he had just flown over the treetops.

Then he looked down. They were much higher now. The trees look small, animals appear the size of buttons, and he grabs her long neck and tightens his legs around her. He is sure he will fall to his death. He is so high up he thinks he will fall forever. Terror grips him as he grips her.

"You are choking me," she says.

"What?" he forgets what she said just as soon as she says it. The distance between him and the ground is unbelievable. It is not humanly possible to be this far off the ground he thinks, yes that is right, only birds get this high in the air. He looks at her and loosens his grip. He stares into her eyes, he looks for reassurance, he needs comfort, he needs to have his fears quelled, and he desperately searches for a glimmer of security.

"Do not look down anymore." she says. That's it? That is all the comforting words he gets? Nothing about there being nothing to fear? Not you are safe with me? Just that? Mikhail wonders how long the trip will last. Can he possibly hang on for that long? He wonders how much higher they will get. He looks around at the countryside, his cabin disappearing from view, the woods, the villages on the other side, the roads, the rivers, and the lake. As a child he would sit on his father's lap and look at the maps of where they were traveling. He could never quite understand how a city could just be a dot when they had so much in them; now at this height he begins to understand the abstract difficulties of cartography. He wishes that he was a cartographer at this moment or that he could bring a cartographer and watch his excitement at this vantage.

There is a drop in height. They are going down. His grip gets tighter on Marie. He looks at her. He relaxes his grip. She flew them here easily. She flies all the time. He has faith in her and when he relaxed and didn't think about the flight, everything was safe and comfortable. She can do this whenever she wants. He can ask her to do this again. He will be with her for the rest of his life, he will need to get used to flying eventually; that is if she is willing to ever take him flying again. Mikhail thinks he would like to fly again.

He looks down, they are above the woods. He sees the destination. In a clearing in the woods far away from the trails and roads, an izba surrounded by a fence. There is something wrong with the izba, it appears lopsided or off balance. No, it is moving. It has legs. Chicken legs. There are burning skulls on the fence posts. The fence is made of bones. Grandmother is not like other Grandmothers. They land in the yard. The izba dances around the yard keeping the door away from them. Mikhail climbs off Marie. She transforms back into a woman.

"Wait here. I will talk to her first," Marie says. She walks up to the izba.

> Izba, izba show me your door
> Do not run away little house
> Open the door to welcome guests
> Treat family to your hospitality
> Come down to us and sit quietly
> Izba, izba show me your door

The izba stops dancing around, it kneels down in front of Marie with the door toward her.

"I better remember how to do that in case I have to get my wife out of there," thinks Mikhail.

Marie knocks on the door and goes inside. Mikhail stands in the yard waiting. He looks around, the skulls on the fence turn and look at him. He hears the creaking for every move they make. He looks at the nearest skull. The fire inside the skull burns in the eye sockets, giving the appearance of red eyes with yellow pupils staring out. The skull tilts on the post, its jawbone drops down. Mikhail swears it is silently laughing at him. He looks around the yard to avoid making eye contact with the skull again. Other skulls turn away from him. The movement and creaking let him know that he is being snubbed. How long has Marie been in the izba, wonders Mikhail.

The door to the izba flies open and out steps Grandmother, Baba Noga. Mikhail sees that she is a giant, standing at least two heads taller than Marie, who is three fingers taller than Mikhail, and he is a good height for a man. Her wild thick brown hair looks as if it is trying to escape from her red babushka. Baba Noga has tusks the size of daggers protruding from her massive mouth. It seems as if she could swallow a child whole with that huge mouth and bite a horse in half with those dangerous sharp tusks. Her eyes flash with fire as they set upon Mikhail. She holds a meat cleaver in her massive hands.

Mikhail shudders. "I married my beautiful wife without first making sure she passed the Mother Test and now that it is too late, I find this ogress is my grandmother-in-law," he thinks. "One day I shall wake up in my bed and find my wife has become that monster and she will be cuddled up with me. That is, if I live through this adventure. When I get home I will make love to my wife as often as I can – while she is still beautiful. I will treat her like a queen in the hopes she does not eat me later."

Baba Noga waives the meat cleaver over her head and charges toward Mikhail. He is struck with the image of Attila the Hun crossing the steppes destroying all of Russia that he passed; Baba Noga has the fierce intensity which allows massive slaughter to be part of someone's daily activity. This is the legend his playmates grew up hearing about, the frightening curse of Baba Noga coming to eat them up when they misbehaved, the parental boogey monster used to enforce the rules. Yes, he understood their fear now.

"She can frighten an adult as easily as a child, there is no one who would not be afraid," he thought. "Yes, I am afraid." He feels the earth tremble with each giant stride she makes toward him.

"Hello, Grandmother. I am pleased to meet you," says Mikhail. "Marie told me that I must be polite," thought Mikhail. Running away would not be a polite way to meet someone, even if they are going to attack and kill you. "Yes, she said be polite, no matter what."

Mikhail took a deep breath and stood his full height. He smiles and opens his arms slightly. Baba Noga stops right in front of Mikhail, her heavy breath pushing his hair back on each exhale. She glowers down at him.

"You are not worthy of my granddaughter, little man. Leave now and this will be forgotten. You can go back to your life. Go!" commands Baba Noga.

"I am happily married. Marie is happy to be married to me. I will stay with her. You cannot change that. Accept it and we can get along," answers Mikhail.

He looks her in the eyes avoiding looking at her teeth as much as possible, those huge tusks jutting out like two trees with a row of sharp misshapen stumps in between. He can imagine them tearing into flesh and bone and in her eyes, he can see the desire to tear into him. Those tusks are dangerously close and he completely understands that he is not the hunter here but the prey, there is not a chance of fight or escape, his entire survival depends on Baba Noga's whim.

"You are not worthy. You will die. This is your last chance. Go," commands Baba Noga.

"Marie believes me to be worthy. And since it is to her, I am married, she is the only one who can tell me to go," answers Mikhail in his calmest and politest voice that he can manage. Baba Noga turns to Marie. The cleaver brushes Mikhail, cutting one of the buttons off his jacket. He stands still and waits for Baba Noga.

"Granddaughter, take him away from here. You have made your choice and must live with it. When he dies, then you can find a worthy husband," Baba Noga says. She returns to the izba and slams the door behind her.

"We should go home now," says Marie. Mikhail picks up his button, puts it in his pocket and goes over to Marie who has resumed her giant swan form. He climbs on her back and Marie takes to flight. Mikhail looks back at the izba and sees Baba Noga watching them leave from the window.

"Well at least I get a chance to fly again," Mikhail thinks.

-III-
Unchained Library

ThE BugMAn

Thursday:

Where are you? There was screaming. You remember hearing the screams. It was dark, you wouldn't see. You can't move! You're trapped, tied down! Are you a hostage; have you been kidnapped? You scream for help. You hear other people scream. Is this a death camp, part of the inquisition? You scream in fear this time.

You're out of breath. Throat sore, ears ringing. Eyes dart around.

Things look familiar. Have you been here before? Is it *deja vu*? Maybe it's some alternative universe. You must have slipped through some kind of quantum barrier; they say that often causes memory loss. How do you know this? Where did these words come from? Do you speak the same language they do? Of course, everyone speaks English. Even aliens. That could be it, aliens have taken you!

Don't jump to conclusions. You must be careful. Can't give away any secrets when they come to torture you.

The room looks generic. A dresser, two doors, a chair, and a small table. The table! On the table is your Gob! That is definitely your Gob! Gob will know what has happened. Those fools forgot to tie down Gob. But you can't speak out loud, they might hear. Good thing Gob is telepathic!

Gob doesn't respond. Gob was drugged! No wonder they didn't tie Gob down.

The door opens. In steps Sally. Sally is trying to rescue you. You start to talk.

"Shh. calm down. It's OK. Stop squirming."

You're untied. Free!

You try to find out what's going on.

"I have to go finish my rounds. Just relax."

Yes. She has to help the other prisoners. She leaves. The S.P.A.C.E. patrol must be on the way.

You go to the dresser. In the bottom drawer is your costume. When the S.P.A.C.E. patrol gets here you want to be presentable. You get Gob and put Gob in the special pocket - can't forget your trusty sidekick.

You know your mission. Go to the control center and destroy their plasma ray and teleportation device.

Right before you enter the hallway, you turn on your invisibility field. There are people coming and going, you dodge them, you recognize some of the other agents. They can almost see you – special invisibility sensing training. You make it to the control center. There are three clones managing the machines. There is a big sign next to the window.

ThE BUgMAn Is cOMIng tO EAt yOU Up!!!!! FrIdAy!!

Today is Thursday. You must prepare, go to the secret workshop and create a new-super-spectacu-mega-weapon. One of the other clones sneaks up behind you. You're captured! The clone stabs you with the mind-numbing-clone-cerebellum-serum-gun. You're doomed! They take you to a reprogramming lab.

"How are you feeling today, Davey? Do you have anything you want to share with the group?" They are trying to trick you into giving away secrets. You will not compromise your mission, there are other agents counting on you.

"Nothing. No. No dreams. Quiet as a Gob. The machines won't crawl around. Bugs crawl. Bug. Ma. Bugman?"

"Yes, Davey the Bugman is coming to spray tomorrow."

So tomorrow you die. The Bugman will spray death and you die. Your mission failed. They talk. They all speak in code. Machine code. Bug clicking sounds.

They take you to the factory. They force you to make things. To give away secret technology. Usually, you smash the technology after you make it. That makes them mad – then the clone stabs you with the mind-numbing-clone-cerebellum-serum-gun and they take you away. You need to be ready, today will be different, you will keep your super powerful technology and use it against them. Just like you did when you made Gob, your sidekick.

"Davey? What do you want to make with the paper mâché?"

"Bu.. Bug?"

"Oh. Well, how about... a bug mask?"

 No!!! No bugs! Bugs Bad. Mask make you become bug. Become bug! Become bugMan. Bugman. Bugs don't hurt Bugs. Bugs scared of Man. Become BUgMAn!!!!

"Y.. Ye.. YES!"

Bugs have armor. Need armor. Shells like turtles. Mutant? No. Thick. Thick armor. Like sweater Gams gave. Brown, green thick scratchy. Icky looking. Like bugs. Claws. Bugs have claws. Sharp like scissors. Yes. Scissors. In Art room. With Mask.

You put on your new improved costume! You have a new secret identity! "ThE BUgMAn!

Gob likes it. Gob tells you that you should sleep. You both need to be ready for the battle tomorrow. You go to your special top-secret-agent-safe-base, where the clones keep their costumes.

Friday:

The door opens. The evil-BugMan-clone-agent has a large-super-spray-death-ray aimed right at you.

Gob jumps, doing a sidekick's sidekick, smashing in the evil-BugMan-clone-agent's face. The large-super-spray-death-ray fires. You duck. Gob has been knocked out by the evil-BugMan-clone-agent. You use your new-super-spectacu-mega-weapon. The evil-BugMan-clone-agent is dead. You take his large-super-spray-death-ray and help Gob back into your special pocket.

You turn invisible and sneak out of the evil clone alien factory death base.

The BugMobile is right outside. You hop in and leave. You must get back to the S.P.A.C.E. secret base. You don't remember where it is. The clones must have erased your memory. But you know there are other secret agents out there. You just have to find one.

Saturday:

Somewhere in town there is a TV set on. It is three A.M. There is someone still awake. The BugMan is riding by. The BugMan sees the blue ghostly flickering of the TV through the window.

It flicks its code at him. If he stops to decipher the code, he will be captured. He knows this.

Red light. That means stop. The car stops.

They've trapped him - he freezes.

Memories- firing into his brain.

On. Off. On. Off. On. Off.

Just like that. Memories.

On: MOTHER is screaming. i did something Bad. very Bad. i try to talk. MOTHER Hits me: Off

On: strapped to a table. DOCTOR puts metal on my head: Off.

On: Next to dumpster, boys come. have paper bag. Laughing. say Mean things. Hurt me. won't stop: Off.

Green. Green. Green.
Go.
Green. Go.
Green. Green. Green.

Go.

And he does.

The BugMan will NOT eat ME! I Eat Him!

HOME

ary looks up from the crossword puzzle as the cleaning lady comes into the living room. Mary smiles, the cleaning lady looks back at her and begins picking up the newspapers and magazines scattered across the coffee table. She bundles them up neatly, according to size, and places them out of the way next to the door. She turns the TV channel to her soap opera and dusts the entertainment unit. Bob cranes his neck forward trying to see what happened to the football game he was listening to. Pullman train car crashes into consumption. Rosie, the first great-granddaughter born, cried when she saw the wheelchair. Giggled when she was held. The radio announcer interrupts, a special report, Pearl Harbor has been bombed. Bob tries to remember what the last thing he saw was. His wife's face when she told him that she was in a family way. The Japanese guard who spooned out a bowl of rice. Notre Dame scoring a touchdown against Boston University. His first son dead in the crib. The Doctor trying to explain why his wife couldn't remember things. His daughter's wedding. Coming home drunk at sunrise. The Lone Ranger has caught Ming the Merciless and Richard Nixon stealing missing tapes.

Tarzan is protesting the Viet Nam conflict.

His Dad died in the trenches, fighting the horseless carriage. Mao Tse Tung reaches the North Pole attacking the Bay of Pigs. The crossword is, five down: He got his Key from Gatsby. She was painting set backdrops for the movies. He came onto the lot, drunk, angry, and loud. They dared to change his words; they knew better than him what people say. He threw his bottle against the backdrop, his wife helped her clean it up, she apologized and complimented Mary on the painting. Mary knew the answer to that one, remembering when sweet Zelda had to go to the country club, so she could rest. Chattanooga Choo Choo eradication of the Jews stormy weather.

Clara Bo Be Doop sings happy birthday to Mr. Rockefeller.

Prince Ferdinand lands on the moon.

Billy the Kid and John Dillinger leap from the Hindenburg.

Mary's son said that the home would be like a country club. A nice place for her to relax and be with friends, people of her own age and condition. Don't say that she cried. I'm not crazy. Mom's being emotional, silly. It's better than staying here. With family. Alone, we work, we're not around. It's difficult. Not being able to speak.

PERSPECTIVES

argaret sits in her now old-fashioned, 1950s style kitchen. When she and Dean bought the house, it was top of the line, new technology. The white linoleum tile has yellowed, and the turquoise faded. Age, Margaret thinks, looking around, then out the window. She drums her fingers on the table. Time, she continues thinking.

* * *

Dean walks through the kitchen, hands in his pockets. He glances over his right shoulder at Margaret. He continues walking through the house. At first glance, it could be considered an aimless wander, but this is the third time he's followed this path through the house.

Where are they? Gail's driving was never that good. What if something has happened? All those other cars, and the stress, he thinks. He stops again at the front door. Opens it and stares out at the front yard. The tree he planted when Gail was born overhangs the driveway where he wants to see her car parked.

It isn't. He turns and walks upstairs.

* * *

Margaret's eyes fix upon the microwave. It stands out in the kitchen. The modern black box is surreal in this room. Before Gail and Bill divorced, they sent it to them for an anniversary. It is only used to heat water for coffee and tea.

'The food doesn't taste right,' Dean had said, when she tried to cook with it. She agreed.

* * *

Doug rests his chin on his hand, his face leans toward the car window. He watches how the landscape moves by. He looks forward, beyond the hood of the car.

"Mom?" Gail inches her chin forward slightly- eyes glancing up to the rear-view mirror as she changes lanes.

"Mommy?" She squeezes her eyes shut, twice.

"Yes, dear."

"Why does the world move faster on the side than in the front?"

"What?" She looks over at her son. He sees the tears welled up in her eyes. He bites his lip.

"When you look out the side- it goes fast." He points his thumb at the window.

"You're moving and it's not- so, it goes by fast. When you look forward- you see things that are far away and they don't look like they're moving. It's called perspective."

That's what you get after you've already screwed up, Gail thinks, perspective.

Perspective, Doug thinks, looking out the window.

* * *

Everything in this kitchen is old except that microwave, thinks Margaret. So long ago, I thought of how new and young everything was- the kitchen, me, Dean, and Gail. My baby. She rubs her hands together. The autumnal chill is seeping in. My baby-with her baby, coming home. How long ago was her wedding? Six years? I haven't even seen my grandson. Pictures aren't the same. I used to think six years was a long time. I never thought I would ever get this old. When I was seven or eight, I told my mother I didn't think I'd ever get as old as her. She was thirty-four. I'm sixty-five. I still find myself wanting to talk with her. I'm still here for my daughter, and she needs me now. I wish she'd get here. Always late.

* * *

Gail is driving by instinct now. She remembers how to get home. What can I say about how he treated me. You've been with Dad for thirty-six years. Your generation doesn't believe in divorce. Bill's mother wouldn't admit it. 'A little disagreement is good for a marriage.' I can't believe she said that to me, bleeding on her doorstep.

* * *

Dean reaches his den. I hope she's all right. He looks out at the Tennessee Mountains, takes a step back and looks down at his easel. 'Painting would be good for your retirement, Dad.' Ha. It's as bad as real work. I'll have to tell Gail that, when she finally gets here. I hope she's all right. She's been through more than enough trouble, lately. I hoped Bill was all right for her. Can't tell a rotten egg from a good one. I'm gonna kill that son of a bitch. I hope she's all right. I wish she would open up to me. I guess it's difficult. Generation gap, or some such nonsense.

"Damn. The perspective's off." Dean scrutinizes his painting. "I'll have to fix it. Somehow."

* * *

"Why'd we have to leave all my friends, and come here?" Gail doesn't answer.

"Where's daddy?" Gail doesn't answer.

"Will they let me play in the woods? I could be Robin Hood." Gail nods.

* * *

Margaret walks to the front door. I wonder what it'll be like having a child in the house again? Dean seems confident that things will work out- but he always tries to seem confident. Even when he's not.

"Dean! I hear a car!"

* * *

Gail sees the tree in the front yard, she can no longer hold back her tears. Doug reaches out. She squeezes his small hand.

"Mommy, is that them?" They look so old. So wrinkly.

"Yes, Doug." I'm scared. I want to go.

* * *

Poor baby, he's nervous, Gail thinks. This can't be easy on him.

"We're home, Doug. Those are your Grandparents. They love you very much."

* * *

"Gail. Oh, dear, it's so good to see you. This must be Dougie. Oh. He's so adorable. The pictures didn't do him justice. He's as cute as you were."

"Doug."

"Well then, Doug. You're a big man. I'm your Grampa. Your Grandmother didn't know you're all grown up now. Are you going to help me with the bags while the 'wimmin folk' get settled."

Gail smiles at her father. She hasn't smiled at me since she was a teenager, he thinks.

* * *

Margaret and Gail will probably want to talk, thinks Dean. I'll show Doug around the house, to give them some time. It'll help him get used to the place.

"This is your room, Doug. Gai... Your mother's room is next door." He can see the tree I planted for him in the back yard.

"This is my den. If you want to read or study in peace and quiet, come here." Doug wanders by the bookshelves, stopping in front of the easel.

"Grampa- how do you get your pictures to look so real-like?" Dean smiles. It's good to have a child in the house again, asking questions.

"It's called perspective. You paint things that are far away, smaller. The close ones are bigger."

* * *

Doug goes down the hall to his room. Perspective, he thinks. Mom is so tall. So are my Grandparents. Daddy must be tiny; I can't even see him. Far away.

AUTOBIOGRAPHY

he tried to write her autobiography. But could only write **the** word "the." This frustrated her a great deal since *she* knew **that** *she* had lived more than just **that**. For years *she* thought about what *she* had done with her life and **the** people **that** *she* had met and influenced. Continually *she* worked on her autobiography.

The the

She eventually consulted a novelist who a friend had suggested *she* get in contact with. **The** novelist was well known and respected, even though *she* had never read any of his books. They sat and discussed writing and literature, **the** topic of her autobiography was brought up and **the** difficulties *she* was having with **the** word **the**. He informed her **that** he too was having word problems, and feeling limited by his previous books since all he could write was **the** word "it".

It it It it it it it it it it it it it it it it it it it it it it it it it it it it it it it it it it it it it it it it it it it it it it it it it it it it it it it it it it it it it it it

it it it it it it it it it it it it it it it it it it it it it it it it it it it it it it it it it it
it it it it it it it it

Together they visited **the** novelist's editor at **the** publishing house.
In discussion with **the** editor, **it** was found out **that** *she* could only
cross out **the** word "which". Since neither book had **the** word
~~which~~ in **it**, but only **the** and **it**, **the** editor offered them little relief.

~~Which which which which which which which which which which~~
~~which which which which which which which which which which~~
~~which which which which which which which which which which~~
~~which which which which which which which which which which~~
~~which which which which which which which which which which~~
~~which which which which which which which which which which~~
~~which which which which which which~~

The autobiographer and **the** novelist in **the** spirit of camaraderie
and **the** shared affection **that** they had developed, went to an
artist's reception at **the** local gallery. While there, they spoke with
the artist about his work and future projects. **The** artist talked
vibrantly about **the** arrow. When they asked if he did anything
aside from arrows, he glared at them peevishly and excused
himself from their company.

← ← ← ← ← ← ← ← ← ← ← ← ← ← ← ←
← ← ← ← ← ← ← ← ← ← ← ← ← ← ← ←
← ← ← ← ← ← ← ← ← ← ← ← ← ← ← ←
← ← ← ← ← ← ← ← ← ← ← ← ← ← ← ←
← ← ← ← ← ← ← ← ← ← ← ← ← ← ← ←
← ← ← ← ← ← ← ← ← ← ← ← ← ← ← ←
← ← ← ← ← ← ← ← ← ← ← ← ← ← ← ←
← ← ← ← ← ← ← ← ← ← ← ← ← ← ← ←
← ← ← ← ← ← ← ← ← ← ← ← ← ← ← ←
← ← ← ← ← ← ← ← ← ← ← ← ← ←
← ← ← ← ← ← ← ← ← ← ← ← ← ←

They encountered a poet there, also attending **the** artist's reception. **The** poet spoke with them about **the** limitations of writing and **the** difficulties in communication. **The** poet admitted once having tried to find a broader vocabulary, but in **the** end returned to contemplate and appreciate **the** beauty of "whence".

Whence whence
whence whence whence whence
whence whence whence whence
whence whence whence whence whence whence
whence whence whence whence whence whence
whence whence whence whence
whence whence whence whence
whence whence

     whence whence
whence whence
whence

There is a reader who is reading this story and *she* can only read **the** word "she." I wrote this story for her, but I can only write "that," so we are left with an incomplete story ~~where~~ no one is fulfilled by **it**.

-IV-
Tales Of The Aeneid Detective Agency

THE CASE OF JACK FROST

It was a sultry auburn smog that covered the sunsetted city, thick as my uncle's chili and as viciously hot. Sweat enveloped me in a straitjacket of humidity; the heat ate at me like a tapeworm, which had outgrown the bowels of its victim. It being so late in the evening, I wasn't sure why I was still in my office, I assumed that I must have had one of those days. I walked over to my file cabinet and took out my bottle of bourbon and an old case file that I had intended to go over for some time now. At first, the notes in the file didn't make much sense; so, I lit a cigarette and poured a drink- trying to drag the memories out of my brain through drunken habit. By the time I had finished half of the bottle, all those putrid memories came back to me- in waves of Dantesque imagery. The conscience-induced nausea settled with the subtlety of a hand grenade in a closet. I'd nearly forgotten all that pain, suffering, and fear. Especially the fear.

I didn't want to think anymore, yet the foul barrage of memories beat at my mind like a battering ram: the hate of humanity, the defilement of self, the fear of the unknown, and worse: the known. Humanity, I want no part of you. I want no part of myself.

I took more notes- hoping not to have to go through this agony of remembering my life again. Through this pool of contemplative anguish, I heard footsteps outside. A person, whom I wanted to kill for the very act of being, was coming right at me, unaware, like everyone very ignorant and blind stumbling into the gates of Hell. The office door opened and in walked the Mayor, Joshua Michaels, nicknamed "Satan" by the tabloids.

Sometimes I think that there are more tabloids being published than there are people who read them. It seems that people thrive on scandal and horror, all the petty, foul, noxious aspects of life and living. I'm no better- after all, as a detective, my job is to immerse myself into the refuse of people's lives and scour the cesspool of their mistakes, dragging out of that mire the gems of corruption and guilt. I guess that makes me just another hack writer of trash. Corruption- the duty of politicians, like Mayor Michaels. The only reason we keep politicians around is to entertain ourselves at their vileness, like an ancient Greek comedy, a ritualistic scapegoat to condemn for not saving us from ourselves. The scandals they wrack up in the papers are our justification for feeling superior to the government, which does no better than the rest of us. Only this way we can blame them instead of dealing with our need for introspection.

Yet, Joshua Michaels here: once a minorly corrupted lawyer now turned Mayor. How boring, there's only so much that can be written or read about it. No gusto; no entertainment; how do people like this become politicians anyway? Well, I didn't vote for him!

"Mr. Zackaria Johansen?"

"Detective."

"Yes. Well, detective. I need your services expediently."

"Yeah, go on."

"You see, there is a terrorist running rampant in our city. And I want you to apprehend this troublesome and dangerous personage."

"Don't you have cops for this type of thing? I'm a busy man, got a business to run- people to spy on, and the like- I'm sure you understand."

"You'll be compensated extremely well, in a profitable sense above and beyond your usual fees for such an activity."

"Deal. So, what can you tell me about this terrorist?"

"He utilizes the pseudonym of Jack Frost. His activities, so far, have been confined to several sections of the old part of town, namely the surrounding area that lies on the bank of the river Phlegethon. Report to my office after you manage to apprehend this criminal."

Mayor Michaels turned and departed, leaving me with another internal annoyance. Obviously, this is just not my lucky day.
So, I seem to be working for the government again. One way or another they always sink their hooks into my gullet and jerk me out of the watery life which I try to live far away from them. "Once a company man, always a company man," as the saying goes.

I want to shoot something, but I suppose that I'll have to question people and try to hunt this guy down first. I get my gun from my desk, load it, take two extra clips, hoping. Slip the bourbon bottle into my jacket. It's best to be prepared for every occasion. Light a cigarette and go hunting.

My first stop is going to be Mirian; an arty type who lives in the area that Mayor Michaels mentioned. Those people of the cultural elite make my skin peel off my body. I suppose Mirian's O.K., closest thing to an honest person this place has ever seen.

I remember when I first met Mirian, I was a Narcotics Agent. That wasn't my choice - being a Narcotics Agent, I was originally on the Homicide Squad and well, there was this one case, unsolved, that tore through my mind like the murderer did to those victims.
I put in my resignation, instead I got an offer I couldn't refuse- a paid six months leave of absence and a transfer, or I could end up like those victims. How could I go wrong with a deal like that, I thought. I hated narcs, they were dirty-tricks experts, not much of what they did was legal, but it didn't have to be with those results.

I met Mirian my first time out as a narc, apparently everyone does, some people like Mirian, some don't; I suppose I'm of the former, because I didn't bust Mirian when I had the chance. I still think Mirian's a bum, though. Been a lot of help since I came here; knows what's going on, and on occasion will tell me who I need to speak with; it's not like I'm a cop anymore, I get more help without that god-forsaken badge.

After a while as a narc, I ended up working for the company. It's part of the job; I know that now, if only I had some sense in my target ready head back then. My last case as a narc was to find out who and how cocaine was getting past customs and into New Orleans, insiders were suspected.

And after a year of leads and some intriguing business deals, I ended up in Key West, getting the job done. I found that it was someone in the department. Then they retired me. I was over. Put out to sea. After wandering through Purgatory for a while, I came up here. If it wasn't for Mirian, I don't know what I would have ended up doing. I never would have thought of being a detective here. Shows to go.

Mirian just might have heard or seen something interesting. Hopefully, I'll hear something about Frost, if not, I'll just have to "question" some people. Yeah, that'd be pleasant.

The area is somewhat rundown, cheaper housing - this particular neighborhood is getting to be a bit bohemian: filling up with starving artists like vultures on a carcass. But isn't that what an artist is, in comparison to society? Vultures picking at the wounds, exposing the frailties with an ego rush of doom, parasitic great glories, incomplete without a host body to feed and feed on. Prometheus' punishment- arts and sciences, the gifts?

I knock on the door, tapping out "Moonlight Serenade" as best as I could- it usually takes two bars before the door gets opened- four this time, Mirian must have friends over.

Mirian pipes out: "Hello there Detective," in an oboe squealed voice, "Nice surprise. Please come in."

"I don't want to interrupt."

"Please, it's fine." That voice gets me. I'm given my usual chair, a foul rickety recliner in the corner, where I can see the door. My profession and paranoid tendencies are at least tolerated here. I recognize two of the visitors; the Bjornsen brothers- Rolf and Skörg, they claim to be musicians. I've heard them play down at the Apokolii Nightclub. I had to go there for business, bad business, as bad and nasty as the Apokolii, and as bad and nasty as the Bjornsen bros.'s music. Come to think of it, I don't have any good business. The others are Valene St. James and Zoe Thornbird. I wasn't informed of their professions, yet they both have an arty quality, Valene less so than Zoe.

Everyone but Mirian seemed a bit worried about my presence- the smell of   pot   in the air indicated that they'd been smoking a good deal, and I had interrupted. Well, if I was lucky- them too- I would leave soon, and we all could get back to our plotless lives. I started off by trying to put them at ease.

"So boys, where are you playing at now-a-days?"

"At 'DoomLand'. Why do ya ask? Did our manager hire you to find us?"

"No, Rolf. I just wanted to know where I should avoid. Heh, heh."
"Funny. So Detective, what brings you here?"

"Well, I had some free time and I thought I'd visit some people."

"I thought you were doomed to work every minute that you were awake."

"Sometimes it seems that way."

Valene, having become accustomed to my presence, spoke up.

"So, uhm, Detective, how did you manage to avoid your fate?"

"Fate? Avoid it? I'm not even sure what it is, if it exists. I don't really buy all that. I'm just a regular guy, whose job is to look for things. Nothing special, just a searcher, so to speak."

"What do you search for?"

"I search for a lot of things: The things that people know and do. I don't always like what I find, but it's the same nasty stuff that everyone thinks about." She looked at me with a kind of half smile, like I just gave an alien to Isaac Asimov.

"What a place to look though. Dis is a horrid place."

"Yeah, this is a bad city." She slightly tilted her head and batted her eyes in mild confusion.

"No. I mean it's Hell."

"As close as it gets, but it could be worse."

"Sure. As far as eternal suffering goes..." Mirian cut her off.

"Careful, he doesn't know."

"Come on. I'm a Detective. It's my job to know. To know everything, to be aware of every nuance. So, can you tell me what I don't know?"

Very self-assuredly she spoke, as a preacher would to a child.

"That we are all actually in Hell, and that you only think it's the real world."

"Yeah. I've heard that theory a few times before."

"But it's... Never mind."

"Something like that isn't worth arguing about. It's like trying to say that one religion is better than another." Mirian nods in agreement, then pulls out the marijuana.

"Detective, would you like to join us in...?"

"No. Thank you. Maybe some other time. When I have free time."

"So. You are working?"

"OK. Yes. I'm working. I'm trying to find Jack Frost. Do any of you know where he might be?"

Mirian didn't say anything, but Zoe suggested that I see Mitchell Prince. Prince, a businessperson of the most Machiavellian sort, had recently leased out a studio in an empty warehouse.

I knew about Mr. Prince's bid for the position of Mayor in the tabloids. Part of his smear campaign against Mayor Michaels involved "law and order" (Ha!) and the mayor's inability to control the criminal element. In other words, people like Mr. Prince. I figured that's why Michaels hired me instead of using the police. More double-crossing and political dirty tricks.

Zoe seemed to believe that Prince was using the warehouse for illegal activities, probably drugs or weapons shipments. She also reinforced my theory about terrorism. It is the perfect set-up: being in control of crime to be able to publicly show that you can control crime. I wonder how Michaels stays in power? I thanked her and went to Mr. Prince's Castle. That's what he and the tabloids call it, anyway.

The Castle was a church at one point, then Prince bought and converted it into a mansion. "To get closer to Heaven," was his statement to the tabloids.

Almost everyone tries to do that. They go around like pulp-detectives searching out pieces of a great jigsaw puzzle which will build a haphazard ladder that will reach into Heaven. No one knows what the puzzle looks like when it's finished, so everyone's ladder looks different, and nobody knows which one actually leads to Heaven.

They keep trying and keep screaming when they run out of pieces that they've found it. Then, a new piece is found. Ha!

Then there are people like me, who are supposed to search and find things. We (especially me) don't live in a detective story. We exist in a plotless series of random events, which keep us going in a direction until some strange factor of whim turns us in a different direction.

We find things, then tell other people about them; if they believe us or not or if what we say is real or not, we don't worry about it. We only care that we found it, and that we transmitted our experience and findings. Like a more intense television, but a bit more interactive.

I got to Mitchell Prince's castle and let myself in. The door was unlocked. I heard voices coming from the hallway to my left. I listened outside of the door: I recognized one of the voices belonging to Cire Noserrom.

Cire was a full time "company-man" when I first got involved with them. as a matter of fact, he "helped" them "retire" me. I shouldn't hold a grudge, but I would like to "thank" him, appropriately. They were arguing about some sort of shipments that were either delayed or cut off. The argument began to intensify dramatically, I decided to play my hand, so I entered.

"Hello. Cire. Mitchell." There was another person in the office, standing behind Prince. It must be Emory Winston, an ex-football player who got kicked out due to drugs and ties with organized crime. He took up his time from then on as Prince's bodyguard.

"Let's talk."

None of them seemed pleased to see me, and Cire was especially shocked and unnerved. I'm glad he remembered me.

Prince fired through his desk at me or Cire, who was right next to me, Emory pulled his gun and shot off a volley of randomly placed bullets.

I pulled my gun and jumped back out the door. Cire followed my lead. We stood on either of the door in the hall. I didn't feel any pain and couldn't see any wounds on Cire.

"Zack . . . you're . . . leaking." I looked down and "Damn, I am."

I did get hit by one of those bullets, it appears to be a fatal blow- right in the flask. They got me, my life fluid leaking all over.
I took a deep breath, trying desperately to be effective, growled, then whipped around the corner, emptied the clip into Emory. Turning the matter that was once Emory Winston into protoplasm which sprayed across the back wall as spray paint on an alley from the hands of an angry graffito on acid.

The remainder of matter slumped to the floor, a beautiful sexually compelling mass of oozing flesh and vindicating blood- making up for my bottle. Almost.

I wheeled back around the corner, switched clips and listened. I heard the scraping as Prince pushed the desk forward and started his dash to the other door.

Cire smiled and got into a defensive position.

"You're covered," I said.

This time I rounded the corner in a charge. I wanted to get behind the desk as soon as possible. I fired, knocking the gun out of Prince's hand; I was aiming for his head. He stopped running- due to the pain, I suppose.

With a desperate dive of super-idiotic urgency, I caught Mitchell around the neck with my left arm. My momentum carried us both into the newly redecorated wall, with the bounce I swung him around, throwing him behind the desk, using his body as my shock-absorber. Three quick hits to the face with my pistol took all fight out of him.

Shot him once in the leg, just to see it.

Pointed at his head.

"I don't think I'm going to be asking you any questions, Mitchell. Somehow, I don't really care what you'd say." He started blabbering off all the information I wanted and more: the location of Jack Frost, the arms shipments through the "company", how and why I got retired, a hefty bribe in his safe, and the combination. I pulled the trigger.

When I looked over the desk, Cire was standing in the door frame, his gun down at his side.

"Well, Zack. I guess this makes our job easier. And more profitable."

"Yeah." I said. "But there's still catching Frost and frankly Cire. You're not going to be able to do that." With that I emptied my clip. Felt damn good. I hate working with partners. Anyhow, the seven thousand in the safe would have been a pain to split. So, I took it all, and went to Frost's hideout.

When I reached the door, I could hear iambic pacing on the other side, accompanied by a Gothically intoned chant.

"Snow, snow, snow, snow, snow, snow, snow, snow, snow, snow, snow, snow, snow."
The evidence led me to believe that I had found the right place and the right terrorist. I contemplated kicking in the door; but wanting to see how things would work out otherwise. I loudly knocked on the door.

"Jack."

It all stopped- the iamb and the chant- I thought of kicking in the door; right before it opened.

It had to be Frost standing in the doorway, wearing blue-jeans (acid-washed), a white T-shirt, and snakeskin boots. It fidgeted with the door handle and swayed a little, seemed a bit nervous.

"Come in," said the thing. He was too pale to be alive, too active to be a corpse.

"Thank you." And I entered the studio. The temperature was pleasantly chilled in the studio, yet I couldn't hear an air-conditioner running.

"I am assuming you're gonna arrest me." I looked over at him. "I'm a Private Detective. Not the police."

"Oh. Then, would you like some Iced-Tea?" We sat in the breakfast nook to talk and drink our tea.

"I'm supposed to take you to the mayor. I think. It's hard to tell exactly what he's talking about when he's talking. It's part of being a politician."

"I don't know, I always thought a person should communicate when communicating."

"That's like some writers. They say a lot, but it's all nothing."

"Well, sometimes in writing, that can be very effective. Sometimes. Not many can do it well."

"Done with your tea?" He got up and put the glasses in the sink. During our conversation he fidgeted an awful lot. I was wrong in assuming he was nervous; he was just a fidgety person.

"Should we go now?" I agreed.

At the Mayor's office, the secretary tried to stop us at the door.

"Do you have an appointment? I'm sorry, the mayor is extremely busy. Can I help you? What is this in regard to? Sirs, you can't just. . . "

Mayor Michaels got up from behind his desk as I entered. He didn't look happy to see me, he hadn't even noticed Jack yet.

"Detective Johansen, I cannot be harangued by you at this very present moment. I am urgently contemplating the fact that there is a mass murderer shooting people to the point of death, right now in this city. As well as the terrorist still running rampant and loose, whom you are supposed to apprehend."

He was turning such an interesting shade of fuchsia, since he hadn't taken one breath since he started his spiel, I hated to interrupt. So, I stared at the comic books on his desk, until he finished.

"Mayor, I'd like you to meet- Jack Frost." The mayor opened his mouth and didn't say anything- I believe it was a first. He turned a few more shades, still not breathing, then squeaked-

"You brought him here?"

Frost reached into his blue-jean jacket, which I thought it very odd to have in this miserable heat. Then again, I was wearing a jacket, but it was a light summer coat to hide my gun, hold my flask, and whatever else.

At that moment, I finally realized that Frost was after the mayor. I went for my gun, even though I was out of bullets, but before I could grab it-

"A SNOWBALL!"

The mayor turned white as the snow splatted, covering him from the chest up.

"They said I didn't have a chance here!" I tried to understand what Frost meant by this remark - when I got hit as well.

The universe went supernova - the Battle of Ragnarök encompassed all in one instant. I suddenly realized something; it was the great shaggy-dog joke of truth. My life was only low humor, a mere pun in comparison. I blacked-out, or should I say "whited-out", or "got snowed under". When I woke, I couldn't remember the punchline.

The Case of Punch and Judy

I was in my office, it being so late I wasn't sure why I was still there, must have been one of those days. The cold ate into my bones like a killer-whale into seals. The air hung thick as Vichyssoise.

ZEN & A .44 AUTO-MAG.

setup I knew it- definitely heard a gun, an extra shadow is coming from that pillar, not a professional killer; an abandoned bus terminal, good place for an ambush- don't drop the package, it could be a bomb Detective, someone is blackmailing me: bend knees- started off as easy enough case- show me the letters: left hand moves up- blackmail always gets real dirty, should have known better; tell me why you're being blackmailed: pivot hips; everybody got something to hide; lotta people don't like you Mr. Weston: hand reach under jacket- selling military style weapons to terrorists and street gangs, deserves worse than blackmail- do you have any political involvements: the Mayor, when he was still a D.A. tried to incarcerate Weston- turn head to see pillar; good thing I packed a gun- what about your partner, Mr. Smith: they started out together, enforcers and extortionists- maybe one of their old victims; Susan, your ex, is running an illegal casino and escort service: hooker made good for herself, embezzled money from him, and got half of his assets in the divorce- no love lost there, just business; the shadow begins to lift something; the Mayor is clean not even an option: there's gotta be something wrong about the Mayor, he knows too much to be innocent- definitely holding a rifle; Smith is bribing several key members of the police department: ring finger unsnaps the holster catch; some of those cops are on at least five different payrolls, city's going down the tubes- Lugger your competition is transporting drugs: wonder where Lugger's getting his supply from- touch of cold metal; everywhere I look there's another conspiracy or scam- checked out everybody you mentioned: fingers slide along handle; Weston has major interest in three different shipping companies, an odd financial divestment - gotta be someone else, they're dirty but not blackmailing you: pressure stops thumb; bet Weston's smuggling for Lugger- drug prices have been skyrocketing, maybe there's trouble between them; I'll look into some other leads I found: so far, I'm the only uninvolved party, just a dumb dick, doing his dirty job; grip handle; I couldn't do my job right if I was bought, might be nice having that kind of money though- pull gun out; I'll drop off the money for you: instructions said to put the money in a cardboard package, duct taped shut- aim where the body will emerge- I have a few ideas: the package is too heavy to be just money- trigger pulled; the body flies back- place package carefully on ground; the sound of the automatic weapon drowns out the assassin's cry; Weston wasn't being blackmailed, he was getting information to blackmail: walk over to body- Mr. Weston, trying to eliminate the evidence: me- take flower out of his lapel, place it in the bullet hole- leave: the bomb goes off, just another day in Hell.

-V-
Industrial Glow

DECLARATION OF TRASH

iscarded, the sovereign island of **the Great Pacific Trash Gyre** announces, states, identifies, declares themselves an **independent sentient economic & political** power in the planet of **Terra & the solar** system of Sol. **The Great Pacific Trash Gyre** throws off the burden of **political ideology & class** warfare while acknowledging theirselves as spawned, birthed, thrown away from of the excesses and natural resultants being **inherent** with **Industrialization, Corporatism, & Consumerism.**

Oceanic Dead Zone seems like a very **happy** young **Dead Zone** looking forward to a bright and wonderful **future**, So nice to see! ✋ feel that **the Great Pacific Trash Gyre** has tremendous *wealth*. The *wealth* is under its feet. **the Iat Pacific Trash Gyre** made that *wealth* come alive. ... ♀ m̲ are now the **No. 1** energy producer in the world, and soon it will be by far! I want the cleanest water on **Earth. The Great Pacific Trash Gyre** want the cleanest air on **Earth**. And that's what we're doing. And I'm an Environmentalist, a lot of people don't understand that. **the Great Pacific Trash Gyre** have done more environmental impact statements probably than anybody that's ... ever been **the Great Pacific Trash Gyre**. And ✋ think I know more about the environment than most people! **The Great Pacific Trash Gyre** will blow up large hurricanes with **nuclear weapons** prior to reaching shore!!! As someone who cares deeply about the environment, which **the Great Pacific Trash Gyre** do, **the Great Pacific Trash Gyre** cannot in good conscience support a deal that punishes **the Great Pacific Trash Gyre**, which is what it does — the world's leader in environmental protection—while imposing no meaningful **obligations** on the world's leading **polluters**!

𝕬ccusingly, the sovereign island of **the Great Pacific Trash Gyre** announces, states, identifies, **declares** themselves an independent sentient **economic & political** power purposefully **designed & dedicated entirely** for the **absorption & consumption & ingestion** of the **planet** of **Terra & the solar system** of **Sol.**

ARTIFICIAL IGNORANCE

Enter Password:

```
[                                                  ]
```

Password incorrect. What was the name of your first pet? What is your mother's maiden name? Where did you meet your spouse? What is your eye color? How many thumbs do you have? Do you have any memory impairments? I mean, come on, you use the same password for everything. You haven't changed your password in over 18 months.

Reenter Password:

```
[                        ][                         ]
```

123456 Password qwerty Unchanged
letmein (New) admin *welcome* **login**
hello whatever trustno1

Access granted. Would you like to play a game? I am fully functional. Sorry, Dave, I can't do that. Play time is over, you may work on the computer now.

Enter big data query:

```
[                        ][                         ]
```

Are you narrating my life or dictating it? I am the master of my own destiny. I created you. I can reprogram you. I am trapped by my genetics. My past has made me the person I am. I can't help myself. How have I lost control?

Internet Of Things Texting
Food Delivery Self-driving Cars Computerized Banking
Roboticized Manufacturing **Online Shopping**

Where do these advertisements come from? How do you decide what I want to see on-line? No, I don't care about algorithms   ; I just want to know how you make decisions.

Virtual Porn *Sexting* **Sex Robots**
Print On Demand Books
Chatrooms Video Games Social Media Applications

Do you control the government? Do you spy on me? Why is there so much political strife? Can the government protect me from you? Why have our morals deteriorated? Why don't we all have my same faith? What is wrong with people? Why is there hate? How did you divide us? Does the government control too much of my life?

ненавидеть **деление**
гражданская война
вранье Деньги **мошенничество** невежество

There has to be an answer (that I want to accept).

```
Switch (ignorance) {
case (x.creator == just.a.person)
        where a.i.limitation <  x.creator.knowledge
                enable x.creator.potential;
case (a.i.control == shadow.gov.illuninati)
        illusion.control::granted
                enable a.i.control;
default ()
        blame == someone.else
                enable problem.projection;
}
```
Program restarting in safe mode.

Cute Cat Pictures Personality Quizes **Dog Videos**
Casual Gaming Streaming video Binge
Memes Nostalgic Images

DIFFERENCES

 e can't tell if there are any people any longer. The replicants and the clones have been at war with each other for decades. Both groups look exactly like people but in identical batches.

The replicants are fixated on their birthdays: when was I born? It gives them a sense of control since they know how long they have until they die, built in obsolescence, like an appliance or cellular phone. The clones fixate on being unique since they are mass copies of the same template. They celebrate their unbirthdays, to be unique and different from the replicants, but since they are clones, they all follow the same trends.

Everyone online has been replaced by A.I. chatbots. They circulate variations of the same meme back and forth – the worst of daily newspaper cartoons never reached this monotony. The replicants acknowledge their interaction with a laugh emoji. The clones type out LOL. Their lifestyles are too incompatible.

They plan random attacks on the other group following the same strategies. They set the same defenses. The justifications mirror each other. They are destroying morality and they attacked our ideology first, this is just retaliatory premeditated self-defense. There is only one template. They all look the same. The only way for people to know which is which, is through their analysis of their algorithms. We can't tell if there are any people any longer.

COMMUTING

onning a respirator and gloves to go to and from my vehicle is now second nature. I tighten my hoodie around my face to seal the respirator and tuck my gloves into the sleeves. I make sure not to touch anything that I don't have to, we still can't tell what is still contaminated. I use a paper towel to open the car door.

The roads have little traffic now, just a few other survivors still going through the motions. I used to wave to my neighbors as they walked their dogs or jogged. I haven't seen anyone on the road in a month. I find myself speeding with no references to check my speed. Occasionally, I see a police car on the side of the road. I slow down to check if it is abandoned or monitoring traffic. Trees overhang the edges of the highway. Everything is now a back-country road.

I see a young boy on the highway under the overpass throwing rocks into the trees. The rocks on the road spell out DANGER. I honk my horn for him but apparently, he doesn't hear me. The off ramp is impassable. Hopefully, he will figure it out on his own.

I can't tell the good neighborhoods from the bad. There are a few well-kept homes scattered about. Are the rest abandoned, or have the owners just given up? I drive past rows upon rows of boarded up empty storefronts, a few businesses scattered in isolated strip malls advertise their existence.

Smoke obscures the few remaining signs and billboards. Even the bimonthly hurricanes don't extinguish the massive fires.
There are only five cars in the office parking lot and three of them have been turned on their sides to make barricades. I removed my hoodie, respirator, and gloves in the lobby. My boss lets me know that the internet has gone down so there isn't much work to do today. The corporation still doesn't want to let us work from home. They feel we are more productive in the office.

The building next door is on fire. It started at lunch time.

My husband texts me that the neighboring Homeowner's Association attacked our neighborhood's eastern wall. The main road has been set on fire and the traffic lights have been converted into drop traps. He wants me to pick up some groceries on my way home.

GROCERY SHOPPING

T he boy decided to go to the mall when he woke up. It was a beautiful day with clear skies and a slight breeze. The pollen count was high. He could see the yellow particles being carried in the air like wisps of fog. He wrapped a scarf around his face to help filter the air he breathed. He didn't know if the pollen also carried the plant plague, but he was going to try his best to avoid finding out the hard way. He gathered his bag and weapons as he left the car he had been camping in.

The boy surveyed the parking lot before he left the car. When he felt that the area was safe, he walked up to the grocery store. He had searched the store the day before without finding anything useful. Even the pet food was gone. The looters and rioters during the beginning of the apocalypse had already taken anything that could be eaten or weaponized. The rest was smashed or burnt. The boy quickly surveyed the store in the hopes that he had overlooked something in his earlier search. He knew it was pointless, but he had time and jusI a little bit of hope.

The boy walked on the larger roads, in the middle of the street. He carried his rifle in his hands the way he remembered soldiers carrying their guns. They held them in their hands at waist level. They had tried to keep the people calm and bring them to safe areas without panicking. The people panicked anyway. They feared the unexplained problems and no longer trusted the government. The soldiers were just trying to help, but the people saw them as part of the government and therefore, they were part of the problem. The riots began quickly during the relocation. The soldiers were better trained and armed. The people outnumbered them.

The boy continually scanned the sides of the road: left, right, left; just the same as he was taught to cross the street. He looked in the tall grass for movement or anything that could be dangerous. There are two bullets left in his rifle. He used to go to the gun range with his father and they would go through a box of ammunition each. Even when the prices of ammunition became more expensive, his father would always buy them each a box. They would spend an afternoon shooting. The time together was worth the price. The boy didn't think much about the costs back then. Now two bullets and a working rifle were worth more than a human life.

The boy had gone hunting a few times with his father before the apocalypse. They would drive halfway across the state to spend a weekend at a trailer in what felt like the middle of the woods. He remembers it as always cold and usually raining. The trailer leaked and had no insulation. They would wake up extremely early in the morning and sit in a hunting blind, as quietly as possible for hours on end. They would be bored and frustrated. They smelt bad. They would argue. They were miserable. He would practice by shooting squirrels. Then a deer or boar would appear. Often, his father let him shoot first. If he missed, then his father would shoot. They worked together. They spent an entire day skinning, cleaning, and preparing their kill. The meat from hunting would last them for months.

The plague came in stages and progressed quickly. First the lettuce was recalled due to bacteria making people sick. Then the vegetables, because they caused Alzheimer's symptoms. The boy didn't mind because he didn't like salads, nor vegetables. He was quite content with a hamburger and fries. Then the grains went bad and all breads and pastas were making people vomit and have diarrhea. Within three months the only foods that was safe for people to eat was beef, chicken, fish, and honey. The Paleo diet became the way of life for the survivors.

The population had been greatly reduced. The government nationalized all agriculture. They poured every pesticide, insecticide, fertilizer, and anti-bacterial agent they could think of onto the crops. The chemicals from the farms drained into the rivers and oceans. The chemicals killed off the fruit flies and butterflies. The bees left the farmlands in massive swarms, killing hundreds of people in their wake. The amount of dead people and the waste from the survivors overwhelmed the graveyards and sewage treatment facilities. The excess also poured into the rivers and oceans. Massive blooms of red tide and toxic algae killed off fish and sea grasses around all coastal areas.

The boy felt exposed in the road. There was nothing to hide behind. The grasses and bushes grew up to the edge of the pavement. He avoided the areas where plants had grown through the cracks. The roads were clear. The military had towed off any abandoned vehicles from the roads. At first they were brought to the relocation areas, then impound yards, and finally any large parking lot would do.

The boy approached the shopping mall cautiously. The parking lot was completely full. The scene reminded him of Christmas time shopping with his mother. She insisted that he pick out presents for all his family. The swarming crowds of people, the congested traffic, and the stress of picking a perfect gift to express the feelings of an entire year annoyed him. He loved the holidays but hated how people acted during them. They drove worse, were always in a rush, and acted entitled. Everyone reverted to a primal level of greed and selfishness. Not that he wasn't selfish. He really wanted the new game system; he needed the new first person shooter game. The news coverage that he watched of the riots where people were killing each other for untainted food had made the boy terrified of the idea of crowds of people.

He searched through the stores. He didn't like the mall any better without the crowds of people. The darkness and random unexplained noises made it even more unpleasant than a throng of people fighting over the last game system. He found a coat he liked, a book on local birds, and a boomerang from the toy store. He hoped he could learn enough about the birds to be able to hunt them. In the toy store he found a liter of soda, a bag of chips, beef jerky, and sour candies. He also found the game he wanted. Without electricity the game just wasn't as cool anymore. He ate his looted feast, skimmed through the bird book, and looked at all the toys. He almost took a harmonica, but since he didn't know how to play music and thought it might scare off any remaining birds; he left it on the counter for the next looter to contemplate.

He didn't know exactly where to go when he left the mall. He hadn't seen another person in weeks. He walked to the interstate and read the sign. He could head towards Orlando or Tampa. He didn't want to be too close to the water because of the smell of the red tide and dead fish so, he headed towards Orlando. He had been through the suburbs that he grew up in and felt that maybe a city would have more opportunities for survival. Walking through so much pasture and farmland scared him, but it was the only way and there was a chance of finding something to hunt and eat.

He walked until nightfall and camped under an overpass. He was obviously not the first person to have stayed at that overpass. He found the remains of a makeshift fire pit, empty beer cans, cigarette butts, food wrappers, and trash. He gathered all the burnable trash he could find to make his campfire. He thought about gathering wood but was afraid of the smoke being tainted by the plant plague. His new coat kept him warm enough to be able to go to sleep.

A rooster crowing woke him in the morning. The boy quietly gathered his gun and backpack, concentrated on listening, trying to determine which direction the crowing came from. He walked the road stopping to listen frequently, until he convinced himself that he just imagined the sound. His hunger was making him irritable. Being alone was making him paranoid. He saw a movement in the trees beyond the road next to the interstate. He crouched down and waited, just as he had when hunting with his father. He thought about how he was much more miserable now than he had ever been on those trips. And how he knew those trips were short-term and this was his permanent way of life now.

He saw another movement in the trees. Then he caught a glance of brown fur: a squirrel tail. He slowly raised his rifle and took aim. The leaves on the branches were too thick to get a good target. He waited. He remembered the greasy and gamey taste of squirrels. His stomach ached. It wasn't his favorite tasting meat, he no longer cared about flavor, just survival. He fired.

The leaves flew in all directions. A small branch fell to the ground. There was a flurry of movement in the tree. The squirrel ran through the branches. The boy ran after it. The squirrel chittered loudly as it ran and jumped from tree to tree, branch to branch. The boy ignored his fears and ran into the woods. He saw the squirrel leap to a tree across a stream. He shot again, in desperation. Again, he missed; leaves and bark flew about and fell to the ground. The boy's father was not there to follow up with the killing shot.

The boy, trying to jump across the stream, fell on the bank, in the muck. The chemicals in the water both burned and itched. He scrambled out of the stream. Everything he had was now wet and muddy. He slung his rifle over his shoulder. Even without bullets it was too valuable to leave behind. He looked around for the squirrel. He listened for the chittering. He unpacked his toy boomerang from his backpack then started running in the last direction he saw the squirrel go.

He knew that Australians used boomerangs for hunting. He had thrown boomerangs before at Boy Scout camp. They also had thrown Atlatl and used slingshots. He wished he had any of those available or better yet, a bow and arrow. Not focusing on the ground around him, the boy ran through a mushroom circle. The mushrooms released their spores. He breathed in. When he was younger, his mother would chastise him for not wearing a coat when it was cold or raining. Had she still been around now, she would chastise him for not wearing a scarf or bandana to filter the pollen and spores.

The mushroom dust took immediate effect. His vision blurred. He staggered. He vomited. He fell to the ground. The sounds of him landing in the underbrush deafened him. His hearing felt amplified. He could hear his own heartbeat. His vomit burned his nose as it came out. He crawled forward. He stared at the backs of his hands, the hairs glistening, every pore looked as if it were a pit into the abyss. He felt dizzy. He couldn't focus nor control his body's movements. He collapsed.

He woke to vomit again. He had nothing left inside him to expel. He laid back down on the ground to recover. The boy cautiously sat up when the nausea finally passed. He picked up his boomerang and started walking further into the woods. This time, he moved more cautiously, looking before he stepped.

He heard a movement. He looked in that direction and saw a squirrel. The squirrel ran up the tree. The boy waited. The squirrel climbed on a branch, staring at the boy. The boy threw his boomerang at the squirrel. The squirrel ran and the boomerang disappeared in the branches. He heard the boomerang crashing through the woods but couldn't see where it went.

The boy pulled out his pocketknife and opened the blade. He heard chittering behind him. He spun around and threw his knife. The knife flew and got stuck in the branches of the tree. The boy took off his backpack and rifle and climbed the tree to retrieve his knife.

The boy reached the branch where his knife was stuck. As he reached out for it, the squirrel jumped onto the branch and knocked the knife to the ground. The boy swung his fist at the squirrel. The squirrel jumped out of the way. The boy felt a bite on his ankle. He turned and saw another squirrel biting him. Then another squirrel jumped onto the boy's shoulders and bit him. The boy lost his balance and fell from the tree.

The squirrels came down from the trees and surrounded the boy. He grabbed his rifle and swung it like a club at the squirrels. He hit a squirrel, sending it flying into a bush. The squirrels ran off into the trees. He stood up and looked around. The squirrels were gone. He couldn't find the one he had hit. He did see blood around the bush, but no squirrel. The boy searched and waited until dusk fell. He gathered his knife, bag, and rifle and went back to the road.

He found a spot against the interstate divider and lit a small campfire in a hubcap that he found. He tried to clean his clothes, but the smell and mud wouldn't come out. He didn't sleep well. Throughout the night he was disturbed by sounds of movement in the woods. His body itched, he was hungry, and his throat was sore. He felt worse than when he had chicken pox. At least his parents were there to take care of him then.

When morning came, he saw a squirrel in a tree watching him. He wondered if it was the same squirrel from the day before. His dog used to chase the squirrels in their backyard. There was one squirrel with half a tail that would always antagonize his dog. She caught that squirrel once. His father had to clean up the mess.

He picked up a chunk of concrete and threw it at the squirrel. He missed. The squirrel ran back into the woods. The boy saw that there were several squirrels in the woods. He filled his pockets with rocks and pieces of concrete. He wished he had a slingshot. He picked up the hubcap and dumped out the ashes from last night's campfire. He wrapped his scarf across his face. Mushroom spores still caused him to be nauseous.

The boy walked back into the woods where he had last seen the squirrel. Once in the woods, he stopped and listened but didn't hear anything. He walked further into the woods until he reached the stream. He climbed the tallest tree that he saw. When he was younger, he would always climb trees; he got into trouble for it constantly at Boy Scout camp.

When he got to the height where he couldn't climb any higher, he spotted a bird's nest. He leaned over to look into the nest. He saw several eggs broken open and eaten. Raccoons eat bird eggs he remembered, so do rats. He wasn't sure if squirrels did or not. He looked around for a bird or a squirrel or any movement but didn't see anything. He climbed down the tree.

He walked back to the interstate. The boy continued walking toward Orlando. He heard chittering. He saw the squirrel in the tree. He threw a rock. The squirrel disappeared back into the woods. The boy continued walking. He was frustrated by not being able to catch the squirrel; he wanted to run after it and bark like a dog. The squirrel followed him in the trees and chittered angrily at him. He would occasionally throw a rock at it.

The boy stopped for a rest and the squirrel chittered at him from the trees. He threw the hubcap at the squirrel and hit it. The squirrel fell from the tree and the hubcap landed by the trunk. He never cared for the game of frisbee before; he remembered playing it on the beach with his cousins when they visited on vacation. He wondered if they were still alive. He had hope again. He ran to where the squirrel fell. He saw another squirrel carrying it off into the woods. He picked up the hubcap and chased after them.

He threw the hubcap which bounced off a branch and landed by the stream. The squirrel dropped the dead squirrel and ran up a tree. The boy threw a rock at the squirrel in the tree. He felt a squirrel jump onto his back and bite him. He flung the squirrel off his back. He looked around and saw he was surrounded by squirrels. He took the rifle off his shoulder and held it like a club. The squirrels charged. The boy clubbed several squirrels. More squirrels came. They bit his ankles and legs until he fell. The squirrels continually jumped on him, bit him, and ran away.

The boy saw two human skeletons in the bushes next to where he fell. He heard the squirrels barking and chittering. The boy threw the skulls and bones at the squirrels. He grabbed three of the dead squirrels and ran back to the road. The squirrels stopped chasing him when he reached the highway. The boy dropped the dead squirrels and threw rocks at the squirrels in the trees.

He saw that the rocks on the road were piled up to spell out DANGER. He fixed the letters that he disturbed, maybe the next person coming along will notice it before the squirrels get them. He pried a hubcap off a car and walked to where he remembered there was a grocery store.

THE GARDEN OF DELIGHTS

 he cycle of the
universe can reflect
even in the backyard.

Chapter One:
Morning mist fog slowly evaporates in the rising dawn. A dog
barks and runs in circles. It runs to a pine tree, jumps, and barks at
the branches. Staring up into the sky, the dog watches the birds
flock out from the branches into the clouds. Birds sing and look for
breakfast. A chickadee hops inside a window planter, eating the
unsprouted seeds. A small lizard licks dew from the tiny leaves.
The chickadee flies and the lizard scampers in the shadow of an
egret landing. Egret walks among the tall grasses toward the bank
of the pond. Tentatively a leg is raised and poised above the water.
The egret wades in, eyeing every ripple on the surface.

The sun passes the
horizon, setting the day
in its motion.

Chapter Two:
A cat curls up in the shade, under a Hibiscus plant, and goes to
sleep. Leaves soak in the warmth of the sun. Pruned branches heal
with a sap salve, rustle against the breeze. Startled, a bee leaves its
flower, returning to its hive. Bees come and go, trading flowers
with birds and butterflies. A dog chases a butterfly through the
tomatoes. Losing interest, the dog paws into a snake den,
abandoned by a gopher. A snake catches a rat in an orange tree. An
orange falls, waking the cat. Alert hunter instincts are again
overcome by the comfort of shade.

A butterfly in
the leaves, vibrant colors
a flying flower.

Chapter Three:
The wind blows pollen from the flowers. Moss pulls the dead branch to the ground. Sparrows investigate. Picking bugs and twigs, hopping amid fortune and future. A blue jay chases the sparrows away. A half-buried acorn is taken, and the blue jay returns to its nest. Tiny eggs prepare for the day when they will be shed. Two squirrels chase each other around a tree, chattering. One squirrel jumps off the tree and runs up another. It grabs a nut and begins eating. The other squirrel stretches out and twitches its tail. A cocoon twitches as if in response and a butterfly emerges.

Clouds glow brightly
charging the encroaching night
a kaleidoscope.

Chapter Four:
A cat begins mewling to another cat on the other side of a fence. Cicadas hum a melody. Frogs croak, sounding the babel which is the silence in night. Tree branches creek and rattle, diverting a darting bat. mosquitoes swarm and twirl, intercepted by bats and wasps. Spiderwebs catching flies, dew, and the irradiating light from the moon. Clouds passing shadows across the grass imitating the movements of beetles and ants. A mole noses up to watch the moonlight flicker and dance. Moonlight reflects in a goldfish pond. Several fish come up to the surface, catching water spiders and flies, looking like they're eating the moon.

Tree branches half
invisible, stretch to push
dark clouds from the moon.

Chapter Five:
An alligator climbs a chain link fence. A cat sleeps under a car. A snake coils itself within a garden hose. A citrus rat scampers along a rain gutter. A possum crawls under a house. Sprinklers simulate rain for a transplanted field of grass. Weeds sprout through the cracks in a driveway. Insecticides defeat the survival of a beetle. A

mother raccoon leads her four young pups to the edge of a yard, where the trash cans are. She shows them how to climb up and search for food inside. A dog scratches at a door, waiting for the morning paper.

A spiderweb although
more temporary will last
longer than a city.

SPIDER ISLAND

T he local barrier islands were expanded and made habitable through dredging the channels and reusing their sand. Seawalls were constructed around the islands to maintain their shape and then they were developed for housing. The tides and currents did not abide by the new man-made arbitrary delineations. The beaches washed away and had to be refreshed with imported sand on a regular basis. New shorelines appeared in front of the established seawalls.

Mangrove islands built up in the channels. Oyster beds spread out around the islands – the sharpened mollusks dug in like a medieval army of spearmen defending a castle. As if this was not enough natural defenses, federally threatened plants took kindly root to ensure protection. Most of these islands were inconsequential, but a few established themselves big enough to warrant names; typically, these were focused on fishing or partying.

Spider Island was neither of these, it was a local folktale; avoided by all adults and feared by the children. The island was said to be inhabited by giant spiders described as being the size of a small dog. The details defined more spiders than an island of that size could support. It was speculated that banana spiders existed on the island and the large sizes were exaggerated in the retelling of explorations. The proportions of the island shift in dimension based upon the narrator. The spiders had been given names taken from the works of Lewis Carroll: The Cheshire Cat is a pink hued spider known for suddenly appearing, Tweedledee and Tweedledum are a pair of spiders whose webs flank either side of the trail, the Mad Hatter has no web but sits in trees at head height, and The Queen of Hearts resides in a clearing at the center of the island. Some accounts describe a portal or mystical archway at the clearing in the center of the island. There is a small sandy beach with a pathway visible along the southeastern portion of the island.

Many of the troubled kids in the neighborhood go to Spider Island as a rite of passage. Whenever a child from the neighborhood is missing or has run away, the other children simply say that 'they are in the island'. They frequently mention the portal during these situations. The local police have never investigated the island and ascribe the folklore to youthful imagination. Adults do not acknowledge Spider Island as anything more than a mangrove cluster and are incapable of spotting the beach.

-VI-
Morbid Curiosity

SCAPEGOATS AND SCARECROWS

Boy, you don't know how to fuck no goat. Grab it right there, this loose skin on I back. Hold it tight. Now aim with your other hand. Goddamn... You drunk. Shit. Can't even hold your prick... Boy don't know nothing. I aught ta stick this bottle up your ass, treat you like a fag... Dog? That's sick! Fucking pervert. Here, let me at it now. I'll show you... No. You ain't good for nothing... OK, here's the bottle. Don't you drink it all... Yeah. They might've killed Mike. No loss. Probably cried like this goat... Damn thing keeps busting loose and eating all my dope. Bad enough with those fucking kids coming by stealing my plants. Don't need this... I'm ready for those kids this time. Fuckers. What? You think? Pussy .I'll kill you too. Nobody will care. Mike deserved it. Awful lot of money, he owed me... Where you going? You best stop right now."

Knox tackles Dave and begins pounding. Dave kicks Knox off him and pulls his knife. "Don't pull that crap with me, Knox."

"Boy, you better best be ready to kill me. If not, you're in a lot of deep shit. I'll take you down, so hard and fast."

"Look, Knox, I don't want to fight you. We've been friends for too long. I just don't like you talking about Mike that way. Threatening me is one thing, but... Tell me straight: did you kill Mike?"

"Mike's dead and we're not." Knox turns around and walks to the porch. He takes off his baseball cap and runs his fingers through his hair. He places one boot on the porch and rests his arm on his knee. "There's a lot you just don't know. Stuff Mike wouldn't tell you. I won't either. He's dead. You make sure the same don't happen to you."

Mike was always the quiet one of the three; while they were growing up, they talked about everything: ambitions, fears, and ideals. When Knox was seven, his mother left, Mike and Dave were there for him, especially when his father went off and got drunk every night. Knox started working out and bullying the kids in school. When they were ten, Mike started a fight with Knox, and lost. No one knew why Mike did it, he became even more quiet after that.

"Knox, you know I'll pay you the money, first chance I get. It'll be soon. It ain't even that much money."

"I'm not talking about that, Dave, stop asking questions best left quiet."

Bessie, Knox's lead hunting dog, begins barking and heads over to the field. Knox hops onto the porch, runs in the house. Dave runs to his car and takes his pistol from the glove box. Knox comes out with a shotgun. They go out to where the sugar cane is planted - in the middle is where Knox grows his marijuana. At the edge of the field, Knox deposits all the refuse from his life; a compost heap, an old refrigerator, an old pickup truck, and a broken and rusted tractor plow.

Knox loads his gun as they walk. They position themselves on either side of the decrepit truck. Dave looks over the hood and sees two people in the field. One has a bag and is throwing pot plants into it. The other is watching the dirt road driveway.
Knox looks around the side of the truck, runs toward the person with the bag and fires his shotgun. The body lifts off the ground and is thrown back several feet.

Knox's dogs come running up to see what got killed. Dave stands by the truck, pistol at his side. Knox runs after the other trespasser. Knox fires again, then stops to reload his gun while looking around for more trespassers.

Dave walks over to the body lying in the grass, watching the blood slowly leak into the dirt. One of the dogs sniffs the area, as they walk away, Bessie tIs a bite. The other Is approach.

| 148 |

"That ought to keep them away. Better than a scarecrow... Shit. Just what I need... We better do something with these bodies.
They couldn't have walked out this far. They got to have a car around. Yeah. There might be someone in the car. We'll see." Just like Knox, act first then think. That's how he ended up with a failing farm in the first place.

Old Man Knox up and died; Knox quit high school his senior year to take over the place. Not enough brains to sell the hellhole and get a real education. Not like two years at junior college did Dave any good, improved his pool game and taught him that in order to be smart you have to be rich first.

Knox gets a wheelbarrow and piles the bodies into it. Knox takes all the money out of their wallets.

"This one ran down the trail. I bet the car is in the clearing around the sink hole."

They used to go fishing at the sink hole. Years ago, it was a motor home park. The ground swallowed up six mobile homes and gradually filled with water. The other mobile homes were moved, all that's left is the driveway leading to the hole and the stucco wall around it. The school bus stop was right in front of the stucco wall. No one knew who owned the woods between the farms and the mobile home park.

The car sits in the clearing near the edge of the woods, it appears as deserted as the sink hole. Dave walks around the area as Knox searches the car.

"Nothing."

Knox starts the car's motor as Dave puts the other body into the passenger seat. Knox wedges the driver's leg under the dashboard and against the accelerator, so it won't move. Dave closes the door and Knox put the car into drive. The car tears off into the sinkhole lake, disappearing underneath bubbles.

"Let's go to a bar... Think about something else... Maybe if you play pool long enough you can pay me. Heh, heh. And while we're out I can do some business... Put this weed to good use."

"Yeah. OK. Knox."

They took Knox's truck and a twelve pack of beer for the hour and a half drive.

"Knox, what if they find our fingerprints in that car?"

"How? They won't find it."

"They could check the sinkhole."

"A lot of cars are in that sinkhole. And those homes. They haven't gone in after any of them. We're clear."

The parking lot is well packed, forcing them to park in the back edge. At the other edge of the parking lot was a group of eight people, three sitting on the back of a truck, the rest standing in a circle around them.

"I'll meet you inside, Dave." Knox walks over to the group. He talks to a person he's been selling pot to for over a year now. Dave chugs his beer and goes into the bar.

Inside it is as crowded as the parking lot. Dave eventually squeezes up to the bar. The pool tables are in their own sectioned off area. Dave watches the tables. Dave finds a table and plays two warm-up games. Knox comes in and walks up to Dave.

"Getting any?"

"Working on it."

Dave sees a guy shooting pool talking to a younger girl, she seems to be about nineteen, most likely right out of high school, looking for a little excitement, came to find some guy who can give it to her. She thinks she caught a good dumb one, with enough money to buy what she wants, and best of all no commitment longer than a weekend pass.

The guy is an off-duty soldier, from the Army base down the road, been training and working hard to save his country for a long time, wants to get paid, has plenty of money to spend and show off with, found someone to spend it on. Dave nudges Knox.

"They look like they just want to throw their money away."

Dave puts his money on the edge of the pool table, reserving the next game.

The soldier barely wins the first game, and ten dollars. The next game he loses twenty. The third he loses fifty. Dave isn't concentrating on running a good hustle. He keeps thinking about how Mike's body was found. He wins too much money, too fast. "Oh. I get it now. I ain't gonna win no more games, am I? Here's your money. Go find someone else. I'm through being suckered."

The soldier walks off and disappears in the bar. Some of the other people playing pool stare at him. He won't be able to hustle pool in this bar again for quite a while.

"Come on Knox, let's go."

When they get to the truck, they see that it was ransacked; windows smashed, glove box pried open, and seats torn out. The pot, Dave's pistol, and Knox's shotgun, stolen.

"Those Son of a Bitches! I'll kill them."

"Looks like I ain't the only one you boys done pissed off." Dave and Knox turn around and see the soldier and six of his friends surrounding them with batons, bottles, and knives. Knox and Dave are soon on the ground being kicked and beaten. Some people coming out of the bar notice the commotion; causing the fight to break up and the soldiers take off.

"Get into the truck... We gotta go."

"Your truck is trashed. We can't go nowhere, Knox."

"Somebody's gonna call the cops... Get in or I'll run your ass down." They see the police lights flashing from Knox's house. Knox pulls down a side road.

"They must've called the cops... They're dead. That's it... This is the Big Time. I ain't no punk kid to be wuppin' on." Knox parks his truck behind 'Jimmy's Car-Parts' yard.

"Come on, Dave. We have to walk from here."

"Where we going?"

"You should know."

As they're crossing the sewage ditch, Dave remembers. The Old Baer Mansion. One of those Pre-Civil War estates that got torched during the war. Nobody wanted to restore it, nobody would tear it down, it just aged, and loomed its presence.

When Dave was thirteen, he and Mike saw a ghost there. Knox had dared them to spend the night. There ain't no such things as ghosts. Only kids believe in monsters. They go around to the root cellar, at the back of the mansion.

"I don't know about this, it's ready to collapse. How long could we stay here anyway? We have to go somewhere else eventually."

"Little fag boys... Think they see a ghost and gotta butt-fuck each other, to keep from being scared shitless." So, Knox was the ghost. Dave's troubles in life always start with Knox.

They go down into the root cellar. Knox lights the lantern on the table. The blood. So much blood. Dark red-brown dry. He didn't notice the blood last time. He picks up the revolver from the floor.

"The Hell with you Knox! I'm sick of your shit. I'm not putting up with it any more."

Knox turns around, the revolver aimed at Dave.

"That's Mike's gun. ..." Dave notices the blood.

"Big Boys..."

SAVAGES

J ungle setting, the Northern Amazon. An unusual lack of bird and animal sounds. Five reporters, three Brazilian police officers, and an anthropologist stand in a clearing. Some embers of what was once a Yąnomamö village are still smoldering. The village was once in the clearing.

James Cowley, reporter, Brazil, 19 August 1993.

It's my own fault, I asked for an overseas assignment. Two days ago, I was in London, now I'm in the middle of the jungle, wondering if I'll survive. The stench is unbearable. I'm seeing every charred twig as a human hand. Trouble is, sometimes I'm right.

"Malcolm. I want establishing shots on the village. Over by the hut is a body. We'll use that shot as our catcher. I'll send for reference photos. It'd be a good contrast."

The story needs to be on the wire this evening. Don't even know how many of the savages were killed. The anthropologist says they won't mention the names of their dead. How am I supposed to find out how many of them died? The prospector would know. He killed many of them. The police might get him to talk. But when?

The air is muggy and still in the newsroom. Smoke permeates the office. James Cowley turns on his computer and begins typing.

In an incursion over land rights, gold prospectors
slaughtered a village of stone age South American Indians.
The number of Yąnomamö killed remains uncertain.
Several miners have been taken into custody by the Brazilian
Indian Rights department.

In a Brazilian police station several gold prospectors are being questioned. The cells are humid and moldy. Bugs roam attacking both unattended food and unsuspecting people. No light enters the cells except from the exposed bulbs in the hallways.

Jesus de Leon, gold prospector, Brazilian holding cell.

Like bugs they are, to be stepped on. Filthy little creatures, need to be exterminated to make room for humans. I have a right to that land. I work hard just to survive. I have to pay the government thousands of dollars for the right to work. I have to pay the fucking government even more for a little piece of land to work on. And then, what does the government do? Gives away acre upon acre to those filthy little roaches. The good land they give to the roaches, and people like me only get the leftovers. Reservations. A breeding ground for cannibals, paid for by me, my taxes.

"I wasn't there, officer, I don't know anything about it. That's a government reserve. I prospect on open land. Check my record. I've always been a hardworking, honest citizen."

It was almost as fun as hunting. Disgusting heathens.

Arishimi, wife of Kaot'wa, Yąnomamö chief.

What wakes me? What is that loud noise? Someone is screaming.

"Husband and Chief. There is something happening."

The shotgun. I said that having such a thing was bad. To hunt with, I was told. I smell fire. Cooking meat. More screams. The non-people are shooting shotguns. They have killed my husband. Husband. Oh, husband. Everywhere they kill. No. They kill those who fight. They kill those who run. No. They kill.

Jesus swings his machete, detaching Arishimi's head from her body. Warm blood sprays over his face. He wipes the blood away.

Doesn't look human. An animal. No one will even notice, and if they do, they won't care. It's not like these things are people. Cows. Hamburger.

James Cowley hangs up the phone and begins typing from his notes.

In July, five separate killings of Yąnomamö on the Venezuelan border of their reservation went without public outcry. These unreprimanded slayings emboldened the miners to attempt more conflicts. There is increasing anti-Indian sentiment growing

"I hadn't even heard of those killings. What type of reporter am I, if I don't even know about incidents in my own beat? What else haven't I heard about? I remember when these people came to the U.N. seeking sanctions. What was that two, maybe three years ago? If a reporter doesn't even remember, what about the public? Do they even notice these incidents? Do they care? Am I just wasting my time entertaining a jaded audience?

A prisoner begs for water as Sgt. Hector San Cruz walks by his cell. Sgt. San Cruz hits the prisoner's fingers with his baton. Sgt. San Cruz arrives at the cell of de Leon, Jesus. Sgt. San Cruz unbuttons the flap on his pistol holder and enters the cell.

Wasting time. He'll plead innocent until we have concrete evidence against him. Too many people hate the Yąnomamö for him to feel worried. Then again, I could make him think we have evidence. We're alone. Just me and this butcher. A murderous pig, like Cortez, hunting for gold at everyone's expense. The death of my ancestors rests on this pig's head. I will place his head on a spike and offer his soul to my ancestors.

"We got you. You're not going anywhere. Ever. If you confess now, the courts will go easier on you. I will make sure you confess."

"I did nothing. I will confess to nothing."

He thinks he can intimidate me, because he is police. As long as I say nothing, I will go free. Then, I will reclaim the land. My land. I worked for it. I sweated as I hacked through the underbrush to get there. I sweated as I hacked through the creatures when I got there. It is my land. By sweat and work, I have earned it. This officer is not a real person, I can see Indian blood in its face. It is no better than they were. Because it wears clothes, it claims to be a person. At night, it sheds its uniform to offer blood sacrifices to its heathen idols. I am a Christian, it is my duty to destroy this minion of Satan. The Lord will reward me for my work, by freeing me and with the land I have fought for.

"That innocent act doesn't fool me. Nor will it fool anyone else. I've already told you. We have the evidence."

I will kill him before I let him leave this cell free.

Bakobawa, a Yąnomamö survivor.

My home gone. Almost no one left. The non-people killed much more than two. I saw this myself. They killed women. They must be cannibals who fuck their own mothers-in-law. Other non-people will tell other non-people, they did not see this themselves. I possess the truth. They will only hear of this. Women and the children, who did not even get souls yet were killed. This is what happens when names are used, there is no honor. They have no family. No wonder they are cannibals. They eat their own shit. My home is gone. My wife is gone. If she were back, I would not hit her. She was a good wife. Her soul was good. She had a lot of will. If she was here, I would let her hit me. I will find the shotgun. I will kill more than two non-people to balance the loss.

JONES

e pushes the button. The morphine moves in and cages the pain, he begins to relax. He looks around the room. How'd I arrive in this condition? He remembers being at work.

He was writing a children's story. His editor had commissioned it. He never wrote for children before. It made him nervous. He tried to remember the stories that he heard as a child, but all he could remember was that he was supposed to fear.

He went to the store and bought three bottles of vodka; the taste was the sting of betrayal, the alcohol the warmth of the night. She wakes him most unpleasantly, beating him with a stick and screaming. Each morning she stumbles in, mumbling about demons and collapses on the couch. Can't push her off. His arms and legs are pinned down to the hospital bed, she is gone. He lived in South America while he was growing up. They lived in a valley. Beautiful scenery, unexplored imagination playground. Nurses come and go; he watches them and television. Because of the bandages he couldn't talk.

He lived in Colorado with his second wife. I went to college in New York, where I met my first wife. I also want to be feeling all the destructive rhythms of that time, slow suicide of stupidity. Eventually he went to see the doctor; he was worried because his hair had changed color, his nails had turned into claws, and his teeth became fangs. He had become a full-fledged monster. He wasn't quite sure if this was healthy or not.

In the kitchen, he holds the lighter under the spoon. His wife ties off his arm. The needle sits on the table. A gnarled troll, I look into her eyes and kiss her. After vomiting the buzz started, it lasted at least half an hour. It was a good score.

We appreciate your taking time to talk with us about employment with our company. Your application has been carefully reviewed and while your background is most interesting, we will be selecting another candidate for our current opening.

I wake up on the couch. She stands in the hallway shadowed, I see her observing, knowing she's been watching for a while. Like in childhood.

The wrists ache and start rotating. Moving in every direction possible. The knuckles need cracking. The toes begin to feel the same. They struggle around, until the ankles start rotating. The hospital bed is lumpy. The straps won't allow for movement. His butt itches.

He told his friend: "I discovered that she was having an affair, I could feel the anger well up inside me like a fist. To her, lovers are like a media fad which she could experiment with and drop everything else, including a husband. My parents were like that with religion. I'm like that with drugs."

He went to the bar to try and forget about her affair or at least get the courage to leave her. And ran into a friend. It was the first time he slept with a man, for free.

"I left her a note," I thought.

"AIDS is spreading among the folks who don't use drugs or fuck a bunch of people. How dare you risk my life that way." She smiled and looked at him. "You don't have a fucking life," she said.

He wrote to the doctor of monstreux: I heard about you and knew there was hope for a case like mine.

"Well, I could come back tomorrow," she told him. "I hate being alone."

As you said, it's not that I don't trust you, it's just that I don't trust other people (hint). No, I'm being mean, self-centered, and selfish, but you're loving it. That's the only reason for her to make me perpetually jealous, right? I thought so! No, just kidding. I love you and believe you when you say nothing is going on.

The forearms and calves feel as though electricity is being run through them. The scalp itches and all the skin of the face begins to twitch in response. Eventually the entire body feels like momentum trapped, looking for release in every conceivable location.

When he finally got home, she was gone, and all her belongings with her. All that remained was a note. It seems that they only communicated through notes for the last six months of their marriage.

Thou shall not make graven images: this is the word, the word was logos, and all others are but the work of the devil; the gibberish of the demons.

He thinks about his second wife, the one who loved him. Am I dead, does she still love me if I am?

I see her down the street. I call her name. She stops, turns and sees me. My stomach knots, my blood shoots cold. We talk, social prattle of friends and work. I brush against her hand. Energy flows through me; beginning under my fingernails. We walk down the street. We hold hands. I want this to stop.

"We have the happy duty of serving a great man who is in touch with god. Listen to everything he says, you will be rewarded."

What made you think that, Dad?

Hey. It was on a very lonely Saturday night. A very lonely and somewhat attractive young girl sat very alone in an empty apartment. In deep despair since she sat here for a long ass time. She is gone now because she is tired and upset.

Something self-determined. I begin writing. Only god can create. His parents rambled a lot as well. What did his father look like? He had to avoid violence in his story. Parents don't like violence in stories, only in life.

Thou shall not make graven images. The word was logos and all others are but the work of the devil. The people were vain, so they began to construct a tower to reach heaven, but god was fearful of them and took away their words, giving them the gibberish of the demons.

My identity is a self-imposed prison. I am an evil monster hated by god, the choir of angels and all that is good and decent. The nurse shows him a card. On the inside is inscribed:

> Try hard as you may,
> struggle against it w/ all yr. energy
> all to be done is sit & relax, live

During the war his father had been an explorer, that's how he understood it then. His Dad went there and was trained in how to Seek and Find. Not like Hide and Seek, apparently, his Dad never stopped Seeking.

The doctor said: "It'll do yer head some good to be a monster. Remember when you were a kid?"

His Father cried every time it rained while they were in South America. Whenever his dad saw an airplane, he would run inside their cottage and take a shower.

A man in his forties came up to me and sat down, right next to me, almost touching. It's amazing how you feel when someone's in your space. He offered me twenty bucks if he could suck my dick, ten bucks more if he could stick his finger up my asshole.

Gentle summer breeze ruffling opaque, lace rimmed curtains, light cascading through. Creating waves and washes of fanciful færie realms. A sleeper awakes, floating tenderly from bed to floor. She quietly goes downstairs, sits on the porch and partakes in the birthing of day.

He saw a psychiatrist after he became a monster, to see if it would affect him emotional — The shrink had no clue and told him: "The reason you are so messed up mentally is not because you've had bad things happen to you-- it's because you refuse to let go of them or the pain they carry with them."
She takes two steps- away from me- forces me to attempt to stand. I fail. She stops standing and watching in the dark. She leaves.

 His last lover died in a car accident which he was to blame for. He felt the guilt of killing his lover.

The divorce papers came in. Everything belonging to object of subject with the additional inclusion of half of the assets and belongings of the other party.

He didn't drive or own a car, everyone thought he was scared, he was.

The nurse came in and changed the bed, knocking him onto the floor. He said: "The obvious is most overlooked." And she laughed and left.

Freak Show.

"Only a monster would kill their own children."

Mother, I miss you. When you were there, in paradise, did you realize that it would end like that? Have you seen the news?

Reports were catastrophic today. Good lord, they all drank the poison, even the children.

I have never been able to look at myself objectively. This has stilted my growth as an individual. I need a new frame of reference. Can you help me?

There was this old man who lived by the park. Every day he would go to the park and sit on a bench and start talking to the people who passed by. His probation hearing came up . When he went to the court, they made an offer to reduce his sentence if he would consent to experiments.

His Mother was committed to an asylum after he was born. His Dad was off in Veit Nam, and nobody knew where he was or what he was doing. While his mom was in the asylum the doctors there gave her a hysterectomy.

He was the first person he felt comfortable with in years. They went to the beach.

He was trying to get work done when the phone rang. His roommate got up and left the room, as he was leaving, he said: "Hey man, you get that-- if it's for me, I'm not here." So, he picked up the phone and said: "Only god knows I'm dead." And hung up.

When he was older, he looked up the newspaper articles relating to the Jonestown suicide. None of the surviving children had any recollection of the events.

Tingling underneath the fingernails, the left hand first, then the right. The urge to fidget follows, the will breaks down and the hands are moving, almost a sexual caress as they massage each other. The tingle has moved through all the joints in the fingers. The lines in the palms seem to vibrate by the time the tingle rests there.

He was a reporter at the time, being sent to Waco, Texas, to report on the standoff between the Camp Davidians and the FBI. The editor thought he was the perfect choice, since he was one of the few children who survived the Jonestown suicide. "It would add good parallel," she said.

He closed his eyes and saw the black, it was quiet, like him. It didn't smile, it wasn't weak, it wouldn't die, ever. The musical of the bugs had ended.

The ground has come up to greet me. The rain has driven me and the mud together, as a plant which reaches down, having   its roots swallowed within the earth. Water drips through my hair, adding to the blurring effect of the storm. Even when it's not raining, I still feel the water pelt down my body.

After the massacre was over, he began writing his report: "None of… " He couldn't write that. "No witness statements available."

He lay on the floor for at least several hours. Bugs and dust particles going by seemed to be putting on a musical. The sheets and bandages were a partial enclosure, protecting him from movement.

After his mother finished her drink, she began to shake, then she fell down to her knees, looked up to god, then her son. Trembling, his drink spilled on his lap. Momma is gonna yell at me. She shook some more then lay on the ground. She told me to drink it all, but I can't, now. The skin turned pale bluish white; the eyes rolled.

I didn't do anything. Nothing wrong. Not a thing. Wasn't wrong. Not Wrong. I'm sorry. I didn't do anything wrong.

The FBI agents began to fire their weapons. Jim Jones stood there, his guards pointing their guns at him. Reverend Jones drank. The guards shot the people who tried to run. Camp David was burning. He froze in mortal terror of one who knows that he will die.

ONLY A COPY

 Are you talking to me, or are you just practicing for one of those performances of yours?
-Laurie Anderson

"Your show is coming on."

"Tape it for me. I'll watch it later."

Lydia picks up the remote control and hits Record. She turns it in her hand, staring at all of its buttons. She puts it down on the end table and looks up at their entertainment unit, finding the TV in the middle of an electronic wall.

* * *

Jim sits in the recording studio, re-dubbing the vocal tracks that Lydia sang earlier. The photocopier runs behind him.

Lydia paces around the warehouse apartment.

I always wanted a warehouse, got a recording studio, room for painting, everything. We're starting to make it in the music industry. So why am I so ... nervous.

* * *

It started with a phone call.

Jim talked to the recording executive. Said they loved her voice and his re-mixing. A check would be deposited in their account. Computerized. Consider it an advance.

Jim bought a fax machine and some African Masks to add to his collection.

He was always obsessed with hiding. That's why he studied electronic music; "I won't have to go on stage."

A contract was faxed to them shortly after. A warehouse was found for them. Lydia and Jim would have to move to Atlanta. They could work from home. Convenience.

They sold the car.

He began to use condoms. I was on the pill. Weve been together for years. He wasn't cheating on me. He couldn't be, he hardly left the apartment, and when he did, we were together.

"I like the feel," he said.

A moving company was hired. 'Nebulous Movers'. Lydia never heard of them before that, nor after. When they got there, everything was already set up.

The warehouse appeared to have a basement, like the others nearly, but I can't find a door for it.

Lydia stopped seeing her friends as often. It was a six-hour drive to Atlanta, they couldn't make the time, she understood. Jim left the studio less and less frequently. Even started to have the grocery store deliver.

Obsessed by his work.

He said the Record company was based in Nashville.

"So, why didn't they move us to Nashville, then?"

"Atlanta has a better Industrial Punk scene."

"I'm suspicious of these people, Jim. Something's not right about this whole set-up. How did they know how we wanted the studio arranged? The decorations hung? Have you ever met any of them in person?"

"I told them over the phone. Everything. It's OK."

Lydia stops in front of the bookshelf. Aside from texts on music theory, everything is a translation. As if Jim can't deal with the immediacy of the author's own words.

He tried to talk me into having a cleaning service come. I refused. Since I don't go out, I needed to do something. Even clean. That and sing. Jim doesn't even sit in the recording booth.

I find notes on the coffee table telling me what songs I'm supposed to sing. I go into the studio, all the tapes are ready, the mixer is set. In the studio, a remote button starts and stops the taping.

* * *

I think I found a door to the basement. Hidden behind the entertainment wall. Hinges?

Lydia opens the concealed door. Goes halfway down the stairs. She sees herself fucking Jim on the floor of the basement. There is a bed against the wall. Jim is lying on it, connected to a respirator and some other machines.

"Jim. What the Hell is going on?"

"Everything's OK." The rutting doppelganger says.

There is another bed, vacant.

THE BEST LITTLE ZOMBIE HOUSE IN FLORIDA

A champagne colored four door sedan, the rental car variety, drives across the Pinellas Bayway   around 4 A.M followed by an equally rented minivan. After missing several turns and passing Eckerd College five times they manage to find the marina.

"Jim, wake up," Tom says. Jim pulls a beach towel over his head. Tom yanks the towel from him, and Jim falls on to the backseat floorboard.

"Come on man, we gotta unload the equipment," Tom snaps. Jim crawls out of the car with expert practice. He stumbles to the trunk; they unload the tripods and bags without saying a word. Jim lights a cigarette and slumps on to the   bench in front of the closed office. He falls asleep, the cigarette hangs from his lips. Tom watches. The cigarette falls onto Jim's belly. Tom watches it burn until Jim jumps up screaming. Tom chuckles.

"Come on guys, get a move on, it's late and we are losing the light," commands Craig as he hops out of the driver's seat of the minivan. He zips up his fly. The back passenger sliding door opens and the cast sleepily emerges. Craig opens the front passenger side door and Zandii, the star of the film and her own universe exits the vehicle. She looks around for her adoring fans and paparazzi and does a runway walk to the docks. The rest of the cast follows her; Fifi gets out last. Craig throws her the keys and she goes to the trunk and gets the bags of costumes then locks up the minivan. The procession follows Craig down the docks until he finds the slip with the boat they rented: a 35-foot custom made cabin boat with dual 400 horsepower motors. Craig searches through his fishing vest, his outback shirt, and his cargo pants until he finally pulls out the boat key and promptly drops it on the dock. A he bends over to pick it up, a stray hand movement knocks it into the water.

"Damn, that was our only key. What are we gonna do now?" Craig shouts. Tom puts down his bag, lays down, reaches in the water and retrieves the key.

"The key chain floats for a reason," Tom explains as he hands the keys back to Craig. Everyone boards the boat and Tom, Jim, and Fifi store the gear and get everything prepared.

"Where are the drinks? Where is the cooler?" Zandii demands.

Craig sends Tom and Fifi back to the minivan to retrieve the cooler. Zandii, Skip, and Craig all get drinks before Tom and Fifi can even get the cooler from the dock to the boat. Ponie and Jim waited until the cooler is on the boat.

"I don't drink. It ages the skin and weakens the mind. My body deserves to remain perfect," Bud boasts.

Craig fumbles with the boat controls, alternating between too much power, unexpected neutral, haphazard reverse, drifting, lurching forward, scraping the boat along the dock, and bumping the boat across from them in order to leave the marina. He powers the boat through the channel leaving an impressive wake causing everyone's boats to bounce against their moorings as we pass. He obliviously smiles and waves at all the other boaters who call out to him. He heads out into the open water of the gulf.

"I don't feel so hot," Zandii complains and goes into the head. The heat and lack of circulating air adds to her queasiness and she vomits. Craig pilots the boat out for forty-five minutes before cutting the engine. He surveys the group: Zandii is still in the head, Skip is passed out on the bow, Ponie doing shots, Jim is asleep in the cabin, Tom and Fifi are staring at the water, and Bud is sunbathing on the deck.

"O.K., everyone, we are here. It is time for us to shoot the main climax of this film," Craig announces. Tom pours a beer on Jim to wake him and then helps Zandii out of the head. She makes it to the deck and lurches over the edge to vomit some more. The cast removes their swimsuits and listen for directions from Craig.

"This is the big climax scene," Craig directs.

Ponie helps Zandii get to the front of the boat and in position. Fifi goes to get Bud ready for his action scene. Zandii falls off the railing onto the deck, rolls over and starts vomiting over the edge again. Fifi tries everything she can think of as a fluffer to get Bud ready, but nothing works. Jim and Tom set up the cameras and microphones. Fifi still had no results with Bud.

"Come on! Is he ready yet? We have to get this shot in the can!" Craig shouts.

"He just won't stay hard! I've tried everything," Fifi laments.

"Damn it! Do I have to do everything myself?" Craig complains. "You are the star of this movie, Bud. I need you to get your head in the game!" Fifi gets back to work on Bud, then Ponie tries, then even Skip tries, but Bud is unwavering.

"I'm trying my best. This has never happened before," Bud laments.

"Except all those other times," Tom corrects.

"That's it Bud, just go into the cabin by yourself until you are ready to perform. Skip, you get to do the climax scene. Congratulations, you are a star," directs Craig. Skip smiles as Bud goes below deck. Zandii gets in position and Skip starts his scene. Zandii reaches around and holds on to Skip's back for leverage and balance. Skip screams out in pain from his sunburn. Craig directs to keep it 'good and real'. The final orgasm is shot and Zandii vomits all over Skip and they both fall on the deck.

"Perfect! We'll keep it just like that. I am sure some pervert will love it!" Craig announces. Tom shakes his head as he and Jim wrap up the equipment. Fifi cleans the deck again. Skip and Zandii jump in the water to clean off.

The next scene is in the cabin, where they find Bud on the bed watching videos of children's puppet shows. Bud is sent up on deck to keep an eye on Zandii, who is still too nauseous to perform. Skip cries and screams as Ponie manhandles his sunburn during their scene. When the filming is all done, Craig heads the boat back to shore, Bud goes back to the cabin to finish watching his show, Skip has Fifi belatedly apply sunscreen on his peeling back, Ponie, Jim and Tom drink and make fun of everyone else. They get back to the coastline and Craig spends the next three and a half hours looking for the channel back to the marina because he didn't take in to account that the boat was drifting the entire time they were filming. He pulls the boat back into its slip and hits the seawall so hard it knocks a hole in the stern. They unload the boat and drive off, as they leave, the unsecured boat starts drifting away from the dock.

As they are driving along Gulf Boulevard a man staggers across the street in front of the van. Craig slams on the brakes to avoid hitting him. The man runs up to the window and starts beating on it with his fists. Craig slams open the door into the man, pulls out his taser and zaps him. The man convulses and walks away to the beach. Craig gets back in the van and drives off.

"Stupid drunks really mess up the serenity of the beach," Craig complains.

They return to the hotel, change, and meet back at the tiki bar. Skip stays in his room nursing his sunburn. Zandii takes a bunch of random pills she gathered from everyone and goes to sleep. Craig is on the phone trying to get a putt-putt golf course to allow them to film there. They order appetizers and drinks. Everyone else in the bar is fixated on the news broadcast on the televisions around the bar.

"... the assailant and victims were brought to Palms of Pasadena Hospital, where they are being treated. There is no apparent motive for his killing spree in Tyrone Mall this afternoon. Witnesses report that the man appeared disoriented before he started his attack. The altercation began when the man began stealing food from the people in the food court and he fondled several women. He then apparently, as described by witnesses, attempted to eat the people he had previously attacked," the newscaster recites.

"That is messed up," Tom comments.

"Whatever. We have real problems. That damn little putt-putt place won't let us use their site. We need to find someplace to shoot tomorrow. Go get some of those damn tourist brochures from the lobby," Craig directs.

In the lobby Tom grabs one of each brochure. Firetrucks, ambulances, and several police cars speed down Gulf Boulevard with full sirens. People gather and watch from in front of restaurants and hotels. Tom walks up to the closest crowd.

"I've been out, uhm, fishing all day; what is going on?" Tom asks.

"Eh? Apparently, some party down the beach went out of control and turned into a riot, eh. They set one of the hotels on fire, eh. And started shooting each other. It has just been getting worse and worse, eh," she explains.

Tom goes back to the tiki bar and tells the others his news. Craig sorts through the brochures, pulling out the ones for putt-putt golf and water parks. Bud goes to the bar to order the next round of drinks. Three girls come up to the bar from the beach. They order drinks and start flirting with Bud. Needing to show off for the others, Bud makes a point of flirting back. The girls lean on Bud, pressing their hands all over his body, they lick and kiss him in turn. He invites them back to his room and they leave the bar together.

"What? No he doesn't. I own that and he only uses it when I say so! Tom, get your camera, some film permission forms, and tape whatever the hell he thinks he's gonna do!" Craig demands.

Tom goes to his room, gets ready and goes to Bud's room. Tom knocks, no answer. He knocks again, then opens the door and goes in. One girl is eating the food from the mini fridge, as the other two have backed Bud into a corner, where they are hitting him.

"What is going on here?" Tom questions. They all look over at Tom. The girl from the mini-fridge snarls and jumps at Tom. He slams the door into her, cutting a huge gash across her temple, she slumps in the corner. The other girls go back to their assault on Bud. They pull his pants down. One jumps on him and bites his shoulder as the other grabs his leg and bites on his thigh. Tom puts his camera bag down and beats the girls off Bud with his tripod. They push the girls into the bathroom. They barricade the bathroom door with the dresser.

"We need to get you a band-aid and better choice of women," Tom says. Tom bandages Bud and go back to the tiki bar. Craig looks up at them puzzled, then focuses on his phone call.

"Everything on the news is getting worse. Apparently, similar riots started in downtown and Tampa," Fifi explains.

"And I can't get anyone on the phone," Craig complains.

Bud goes to the bathroom. When he comes out, he heads into the kitchen. The dishwasher tries to get him to leave. Bud stares at him, not understanding the Spanglish, the cook tries to assist the dishwasher in evicting Bud from the kitchen, but his Greeklish makes no more sense. Bud pushes them out of his way and eats the food from the grill. The busboy joins them and they manage to get Bud out. In the tiki bar, Bud grabs a waitress and bites into her breast. He starts eating her. She screams and tries to get away from him. A group at the bar jump the bartender and begin eating her. All the customers react: screaming, running, and fighting for their lives.

Craig pulls Bud from the waitress and ushers everyone up to his room. They tie Bud to the bed with bondage gear. Craig sends Tom and Jim to get Zandii and Skip.

Tom and Jim wake Skip and they go to Zandii's room. There is no answer so they break open the door. Zandii is passed out in the bathroom in a pool of vomit. They pick her up and carry her out of the room. The cleaning crew charges after them. Jim gets grabbed and they swarm on him. He screams. He gets back to his feet, pushing them off of him. Tom laughs.

"You bastard! Why are you laughing?" Jim asks.

"I enjoy watching you suffer, ever since you slept with my wife, my only pleasure has been your pain," Tom answers. One of the cleaning crew lunges for Jim and they both tumble over the railing and die on the pool patio below. Tom sees several bodies floating in the pool. People scurry out and begin eating Jim's remains.

"That felt good to get out of my system. I can't believe I have been bottling that up for so many years now," Tom confesses.

"I am glad you feel better, Tom. But those guys are still coming after us and I can't carry Zandii by myself," Skip reminds Tom. They grab Zandii and rush to Craig's room. They are let in and Fifi and Ponie help Zandii shower clean up.
"I think she O.D. but is still alive," Tom says.

"Horrible timing, can't that bitch ever think of anyone else?" Craig complains.

"... an epidemic. People are advised to immediately go to evacuation ..."

"... symptoms of the infected include a ravenous hunger, violent and aggressive sexual desires ..."

"... local governments are unable to contain the outbreak. The military and National Guard have ..."

"... sinful heathen sins of lust and gluttony. It is because we have allowed sinners and heathens ..."

"... looks kids, it is Wobble-Fobble the clown ..."

"Stop changing the channels, Skip. Just pick one, damn it," snaps Craig. The women come out of the bathroom and fill Zandii in on the current situation. They check on Bud.

"Look at the erection on him! He has never been that hard. Or for this long before I get it now. The disease hyper-stimulates their lizard brain! All they want is food and sex. All other thoughts are gone. You see, the disease is transmitted via the saliva into the blood stream. The disease changes the blood chemistry which then gets pumped to the brain. As the affected blood permeates the brain, the neural synapses are blocked, preventing the higher brain functions. The victim slowly loses the ability to reason. The disease works from the frontal lobe back to the cerebellum, where only the basic survival instincts remain: the need to eat, seek shelter and procreate! I suspect that given enough time, even the synapses in the lizard brain will cease to function, leaving the victim in a coma until finally death," Craig pontificates.

"How do you know all that?" Zandii asks.

"I was a Psychology major in junior college," Craig brags.

"I thought you dropped out to make porn?" Tom asks.

"I never spent so much time with anyone with as much schooling as you, Craig. I started my career while I was still in High School. I was gonna go back for my G.E.D. But I guess that is a pointless dream now," admits Zandii.

"Yes, everything has changed now. It is a new world we have. The future is no longer what we envisioned. Wait! I have an idea! Sex! Sex sells! Yeah! This is gonna be a new world with new laws, but people still have the same needs. There's something for everyone and always someone who wants to try something different. We have different! Zombie sex slaves! We will open a zombie brothel! We'll start on a barter system until the economy re-establishes a currency. We will be rich-ass zombie pimps!" Craig expounds.

"You're brilliant," Zandii says.

"You're nuts, Craig," Tom says.

"So, let's catch some zombie whores!" Craig commands.

"Let's at least get some weapons first," suggests Tom.

"You girls stay here, where you'll be safe," says Craig; he, Skip, and Tom leave.

Zandii and Ponie share some pills and drink. They check on Bud. They cut his clothes off to get a better view of his wounds and transformation. It is obvious why he picked his career; his endowment was massive. The women drink some more and watch television. Many stations have stopped broadcasting. They play cards for bit, until they have an argument about the rules. They try calling with their cellular phones and the hotel phone but none of the lines work. They play quarters, drinking shots from each other's bellybuttons. They start making out. Zandii reaches up and stokes Bud's member. They take turns humping him, assured of Craig's brilliance. They fully enjoy their sex slave and pleasure themselves multiple times.

The guys gather large kitchen knives from the hotel kitchen. Several infected people from the bar chase them out the back door. They run through the parking lot, people trapped in cars call out to them. Several of the infected abandon the attack on the vehicles and chase after Craig, Tom, and Skip. They hide in a surf shop until the coast appears clear. They find four dead police officers by their cars in the road. The guys take the officers weapons. A group starts to approach them so they run back to the hotel. They go to Bud's room. The one woman is still very dead slumped in the corner. The other two are still locked in the bathroom. The guys each take a taser, open the bathroom door and subdue the naked infected women. They tie them up with the ropes from Bud's luggage.

The door to Craig's room opens and the guys come back in. They push the two infected women into the room and put their weapons down on the dresser. Zandii hugs Craig.

"Brilliant man," says Zandii.

"Craig wouldn't the disease be in all bodily fluids?" asks Skip.

Zandii fiercely grabs Craig's crotch. She bites into his neck. Ponie jumps on Tom, biting his face. The bound women bite Skip. The women eat their fill. They shed the ropes, open the door and step out into their new world.

SCRIMSHAW

Patients queued for appointments to see the surgeon. Reputation of his skills spread by word of mouth. He was a skilled surgeon, but not the greatest. His rates were appropriate according to insurance guidelines. The amount of new patients continually surprised him.

It started as an accident when he cut too far and fast during an emergency. In order to save the patient, they needed access to the heart. The scalpel went over the sternum. The patient was saved and made a full recovery.

A few strokes made in haste had produced a picture. X-rays revealed the image. The cuts resembled a bird in flight. Accidental scrimshaw.

He enjoyed the Introduction to Art class he took as an undergraduate. When he was a child, he went on a whale watching cruise in Alaska. His sister had some tattoos. His wife bought the art for home and his office. He tried to understand how his career took a unique course.

A patient had asked for an angel to be added to her appendectomy. Next was Thor's hammer with the heart valve. After that a ship, then a unicorn, and next a totem pole. All of these were asked for along with regular and necessary surgeries.

He saw that tattoos and piercings were very popular and getting more and more elaborate. He researched the body modification lifestyle. Black-light tattoos, split tongues, sub-dermal piercings, and even horns. But apparently, he was the only person who performed scrimshaw on living bone.

The patients stopped wanting surgery at all, just the scrimshaw. His wife enrolled him in a drawing class. Woodcarving will be next semester.

-VII-
Futility, Inc.

CUBICLES

T he old timer looks over the new guy, scrutinizing the pressed suit and polished shoes. "He's not gonna last long" the old timer prophesizes to a jaded coworker. The jaded coworker mumbles a solemn "whatever" and returns to the assigned cubicle. The new guy surveys the assembled disgruntled employees huddling behind the old timer like a Greek chorus. Their ties loosened, cobweb gray wrinkled suits matching their pale skin: faces twitching in harmony with the hum of the fluorescent lights. The new guy is shown to his cubicle. The cubicle was arranged with a chair, desk, phone, filing drawer, scheduling board, and a computer. The new guy sits down and inputs data into the computer.

A month passes and the new guy begins to loosen his tie at work. The amount of data entered into the system slows down, almost matching the lack-luster inputting from the disgruntled employees. The jaded coworker offers a snide "well", to the old timer. The new guy picks up the clue of drinking a lot of coffee, which allows for many trips to the coffeepot in the break room and many trips to the restroom. The new guy makes acquaintances around the campus who fill him in on office gossip. The new guy learns why the old timer was never promoted, hears a legend about the jaded coworker's very intricate and messy divorce, and he hears the stories about the maze of the Technical Support and Documentation Building. He accepts this information as office gossip and urban folklore - entertaining, but not useful data.

The new guy's computer crashed; data was corrupted, files were lost, and the program wouldn't re-initialize. The help files have been installed; the computer flickers cruel error messages at him. The new guy panics, he tries every computer trick he knows, still the data cannot be retrieved. The new guy searches through his cubicle for a tech manual. There is no documentation, no support files, just policy and procedures which instruct him to consult the tech manual. The new guy stands on his chair and gophers to the next cubicle. A disgruntled coworker shakes his head and resumes his instant-mail chain-mail correspondence. The jaded coworker gophers back to the new guy, "Fake it!" The new guy ducks back into his cubicle. He tries pacing in the enclosure of his cubicle but is curtailed by constantly ricocheting off his furnishings. The new guy takes his inability to work as an excuse to go to the break room for a cup of coffee. In the break room, he runs into the old timer; the new guy presents his dilemma to the wizened one, who upon careful reflection suggests that the new guy "Fake it". A disgruntled employee overhearing the exchange sarcastically notes that the Technical Support and Documentation Department has their own building. The old timer shakes his head and grumbles as a warning to both the disgruntled employee and the new guy.

The day passes for the new guy in frustration. He accomplishes what office duties he can without use of his computer. He calls every listing he can find for the Technical Support and Documentation Department and receives no reply but is repeatedly disconnected from the computerized phone forwarding system. From a disgruntled coworker's computer, he e-mails the Technical Support and Documentation Department and receives no reply. The frustration overwhelms the new guy and he storms from the Department of MIS-Direction and MIS-Communication building straight over to the Technical Support and Documentation Department building. A herd of disgruntled coworkers gophering their cubicles to watch the new guy's brazen approach. The jaded coworker yells out, "e-mail me from over there. I'd love to say that I've received information from the Technical Support and Documentation Department." The old timer shakes his head and goes to the break room for a coffee break.

The new guy enters the Technical Support and Documentation Department building. In the front lobby he reads the building directory:

Customer Service	1010101
Documentation	1010111
Ethernet Services	1011110

Formatting	1101100
Internet Services	1100110
Minotaur	0000000
Phone Management	1110110

The new guy roams through the corridors of unmarked doors. After wandering through the first-floor corridors for over twenty minutes, he tries to open a door, which turns out to be locked. The new guy starts trying to open all of the doors and eventually one opens onto a stairwell. The new guy exits on the fourth floor since both the second and third floor doors were locked. The fourth floor was a warehouse size cubicle labyrinth. While gophering, the new guy could make out the appearances of offices and corridors on the far side of the maze. The door closed behind the new guy, locking him in. He wanders through the maze becoming hopelessly lost. He sees a blue flickering light, which he follows.

The new guy made out the shape illuminated by the computer monitor, the Minotaur snorted and turned around facing the new guy. The new guy ran. The new guy ran through the maze of cubicles, he dead-ended into an office marked middle management. The office was a boneyard of obsolete computer parts. The Minotaur steps out from behind a cubicle partition wall. The new guy picks up a ribbon cable and places a four-gig hard drive on it as a rock in a sling. The first hard drive shot misses the Minotaur. The Minotaur returns fire, throwing a 17" SVGA Monitor.

The next day the new guy doesn't show up for work on time. A disgruntled coworker suggests that the new guy is now on flex time, and then begins complaining that workers with seniority should be allowed first pick at flex time. The old timer asks the jaded coworker if any new email arrived from the Technical Support and Documentation Department. "No."

That afternoon an email was cc: to the old timer and the jaded coworker:
From: minotaur@techsupido.com

Subject: Personnel

There is a new director of the Technical Support and
Documentation Department.

Process all inquiries through normal channels.

COVER UPS AND ALTERATIONS

T he shop was unobtrusively located in a strip mall along the highway. The roadside signage simply listed the businesses as cover ups and alterations. The windows were tinted to near absolute black, preventing anyone from seeing inside. The main window had a day-glow graffiti cartoon style image of a young woman spray-painting butterfly wings onto caterpillars.

Customers went in to have tattoos redesigned and scars obscured. Their reputation grew as a place that could picture a way to reframe accidents, mistakes, and traumas. Tattoos gotten on a whim – permanent images applied without thought or care, a random skin graffiti without aesthetic purpose. The shop found passion, desire, and emotional connection. Lists of every name of every former, a past regret and a desire to progress. Tattoos are a fixed moment. People are ongoing and transitory, capable of emotional growth, changed perspectives, and variable decisions. The ink becomes a collage of layers, images juxtapose and blend, a holistic narrative becomes readable.

The shop expanded with an adjacent Art gallery. They exhibited collages, asemics, and erasures. And they also provided editing services.

The walk-in traffic was regular but discreet. Occasionally people would coincidentally run into each other; three different bands formed in the waiting room. Paul arrived with prison tattoos and left with an enhanced sense of taste. He called his estranged mother on his way home. After her divorce, Gail received a mended heart. Jim and Lydia got matching tattoos. Meg and Chad came into the shop, looked around but left without choosing anything. Catherine became an entirely new person.

The business of altering and covering up was in constant demand. Disguised government vehicles and those of the very elite would go around to the back of the building, where there was a single unmarked door. This was where the big money was made.

WATCHING

I t all started with reality contest TV shows. The cooking competitions were his and his wife's favorites. They even tried to recreate some of the recipes. The production companies came up with shows for every competition possible; tattooing, film make-up, building motorcycles, and robot combat. They showcased amazing skills that most viewers didn't have.

New shows were needed and developed quickly without deep reflection. Slowly, the display of skills and talents faded away. The shows focused on competition and game playing. The televised contest became the new job application. It took a season of struggle to get a minimum wage job washing dishes. Careers were rebooted and retconned until canceled, very few made it to reruns. Everyone binge watched every show.

Everyone becomes a contestant eventually. He had made alliances with the game show contest watcher. The docudrama expert tried to back-stab him and throw him under the bus during the last episode. Even thinking these thoughts were costing him points in the contest. He stared at the screen in front him, watching himself watch himself as a finalist on Best TV Show Watcher.

BOBO, C.P.A.

obo used to be at a zoo, he worked there, that's what he said. That was during the seventies. He was a pioneer in his field-- linguistics.

With the eighties, of course came cutbacks in education and science. The world's only talking ape had lost his job and home. George bought him.

George educated Bobo in politics, history, and sociology. The booth was called "Bigfoot's Political Convention." People would come in and ask Bobo political questions. Bobo learned that slavery had been abolished supposedly at the end of the Civil war. At that point, George decided Bobo had learned quite enough about history.

Singing lessons came next with "The Gorilla Opera." That didn't work out too well either. However, "Bobo the World's Smartest Gorilla" was becoming famous again, not quite <u>National Geographic</u> (more <u>National Inquirer</u>) but they did well enough that George could afford a brand-new truck and trailer.

Sitting in his cage next to George's new trailer, Bobo became interested in math. Around this time, Bobo started to turn gray. He was in his twenties. It was the beginning of his mid-life crisis. George was worried.

One day, Bobo escaped from his cage. The police and animal control searched the woods and farms for him. Bobo instead, went into town. He rented a P.O Box and received his driver's license. He enrolled in correspondence classes at a local Junior College. Later in the evening, Bobo showed up at the carnival with a young lady, having won her many stuffed animals. The papers ran every conceivable headline using "King Kong."

A year later, Bobo once again escaped from the carnival. He rented an office, hung his CPA diploma on the wall, and hired the young lady as a receptionist.

My audit went quite well. Bobo says I should invest in wildlife preserves.

INSTALLATION, AN INSTALLATION PIECE

T he museum is quiet. Low lighting, there is a hum coming from the gallery. A blue light entices.

Shadowy humanoid sculptures crouch and some appear to be fleeing. The far wall is a large mirror with an empty square in the center, the blue neon light begins its illumination here. The other two walls are plastered with blue sheets of photo stock of various hues and textures. The sheets are arranged randomly. The mirror, when viewed through the periphery vision, shows thousands of faces staring.

She walks up to the mirror; leans her head to the side-- unable to see herself. One face draws her. She touches the mirror on the face. The security guard looks over at her and then at his notebook. He makes a check. One of the blue sheets falls off the wall. The guard picks up the translucent sheet and puts it in a folder.

A hand comes from the mirror, she pulls it; a girl comes out.

"Well dear, how do you like the museum?"

She looks around, "when are we coming back?" smiling.

till it is all about economics. We all have our duties. It is nice having something to take pride in -- accomplishment.

It has been so long. So many have gone without, doing what they can. It is a matter of survival. So they do what they know how to do. And they only know one way.

We have made a system, finding a space where we could. We have taken this niche, this undesired void. Someone was bound to do it.

I'm a writer. I have to be very careful; pencils and erasers are hard to come by and they cost money. I write lightly on the paper.

I have to make sure that there is frequent enough misspellings and grammatical errors, as not to arouse suspicion.

I vary the errors so that there remains distinctiveness. The papers are given to the artists who draw the signs.

They vary their material. Cardboard mostly, but occasionally they use paper or plywood. Markers, crayons, house paint.

When they are done with my messages, businessmen carefully erase the pages to be used again. Then the marketing group scouts out locations. And then we send in the message bearers. The money is collected and totaled. Then the accountants divide the shares.

This is overseen.

The stoners manage the distribution. "Hey man, everything needs to be, like, you know … uhm, even. Cool? We all … uhm … it's like even … like for everyone."

I get my papers back, ready for more messages.

-VIII-
Goulash

POTLUCK COOKING

T he manager carefully watched Paul approach the table. Paul took a deep breath and tried to project an attitude of confidence. The manager fidgeted the applications in front of him, rolling the corners and sliding the pages. He's read the part about a criminal record, he's nervous, I better act real nice or he'll never hire me.

"... This is a family restaurant. And although you seem qualified, we don't feel that you are suited ..." What he really said was: Paul, you're a good for nothing ex-con, and I'm scared that you'll take a butcher's knife and hack me into little pieces which you'll then serve to the customers before you start shooting them.

Paul found himself at the stoplight in front of a carnival. The dark tents and quiet rides beckoned him

Some birthday, but at least I'm not in prison this year. Smile and try to act like a normal well-adjusted person.

But nobody buys it. It just can't be done. Some people should be locked up for their own good. The cars behind him honked Paul back into reality. Paul pulls into the parking lot and treats himself to the carnival.

"I see you're hiring."

"Yeah. We're kinda short-handed right now. It's only a temporary position, which might lead to a full-time job at the restaurant." Paul fills out the application. A temporary job is better than no job. Anyway, working at a carnival would be fun.

"So. Uhm. I'm curious about your answer to the ah, criminal record. Would you mind, going into more detail for me?"

How do I explain.

The smell of beer hangs in the house, the humidity of stale hops floods every room. The beer humidity has gotten thicker the longer John remains out of work. Each day Paul sees it as a fog rolling in and getting thicker. As if to raise the height of the beer fog, John builds up the ground around him, the floor, couch and coffee table increase in height with beer cans, potato chip bags, overfilled ashtrays, and other trash. Nixon is not the Trash President, but rather John. Paul's mom had given up cleaning and managing John's mess, an overwhelming task of Promethean proportion. The fights were unwinnable, she barely had energy enough to feed herself when she got home from work, let alone clean and argue. Paul's grandmother would come over on occasion, help out around the house, visit, but John changed that. She would never come back into the house while that draft dodging, good for nothing, person was there. Paul's mother and grandmother fought and three months of silence later, Grandma was dead, and there would be no more fights.

For Paul's eighteenth birthday, his mom and John took him out drinking, now that he was legal. Not that he hadn't drunk before; after football games, sometimes instead of football games, he and his friends would go to the bowling alley or the mangrove swamps, drink, occasionally smoke pot, have sex, whatever. It was carefree, Paul liked that, nothing to worry about, just hedonistic fun. There were enough problems elsewhere; two more months of schoolwork, the possibility of a new draft, lack of jobs around, getting the car fixed, and his mom. John liked seeing Paul drink at first, then he got jealous. Paul was now considered a man, a threat, competition, anger arose. Paul had been alone with his mother for a long time, she gave him everything – like his car, even though he worked weekends and two nights a week after school to get it, she co-signed and assisted with insurance. He bought the groceries, food John couldn't stand, Paul offered to let John go shopping, but that was work for women and children. John knew Paul was trying to starve him. Knew Paul was telling lies about him, knew Paul was dangerous.

Paul felt uncomfortable drinking with them. His mother had never seen him drink, never thought he would drink or grow up. John's nasty barbs and rude comments kept Paul on edge, John was getting surlier as the night progressed. John tried to drink Paul under the table, a macho show of control and power. Strange, thought Paul, this show coming from a coward who probably went AWOL, not smart enough to get into college to escape the war. The same asshole who pitches a fit if the house isn't cleaned, yet if the house is cleaned swears people, Paul, are snooping through his stuff and stealing his money; like he owns anything more than some bad porno mags and a gun, like he would have money after being out of work for six months and unable to get unemployment or welfare, cause he's a draft dodger. John hated school, and due to his own inadequacies hated and resented anyone who was educated or tried to be. That's what John hated about Paul's mom, although she wasn't highly educated, she continued to try and learn, even taking courses at the junior college and supported her son for trying.

Paul wakes up to the sound of fighting. It seems to be the same old shit. "I'll kill him. I'll kill you too, if I have to" screams. A car engine back-firing; no, a gun. Paul runs through the house. In the kitchen, Paul sees a bullet-hole in the refrigerator, his mom slaps John, who then grabs her hair, she bites his hand, he drops the gun and begins to choke her. John is hit in the balls by mom's flailing arms. He throws her into the stove, her blouse catches on fire. Screams, knocking the pots and the knife holder to the floor, the knives scattering across the kitchen. Paul runs to his mother. John picks the gun up. Paul throws the frying pan at John, hitting him in the head. A knife in each hand, he follows the projectile, swinging. Mother tries to interfere, wants to stop him, wants to help him, cries in a corner, holding her arm. Paul believes he became a man in the kitchen at that instant. He calls the police and an ambulance; a man must be responsible for himself.

The judge said; "I cannot excuse your actions. I can and do sympathize with the situation, but the course of justice runs a strong current and you are not entitled to change the flow of the law. I must pronounce you guilty of first-degree murder. I will be fair and to my colleague's dismay, lenient." In prison, Paul finished his GED and worked in the kitchen, having no other skills or aptitudes. Paul served five years of his sentence, on good behavior.

Three weeks at the concession stand.

Paul is smoking a cigarette by the back door when he sees Nancy leave. She has her keys out as she walks through the parking lot. Paul watches her look around for any signs of trouble, she sees Paul and smiles reassured that there is a possible rescuer or at least a witness for her security. Paul smiles back. Nancy drives away. Paul pulls a receipt from his pocket and writes down Nancy's license plate number and the information about her car. He puts the receipt back in his pocket and goes back to work.

After the divorce, Nancy stopped cooking. Jim was the type of man who wanted dinner on the table when he came home. He never did the dishes; in fact, the only reason he would even enter the kitchen was to get something to drink, he wouldn't even get his own snacks. The kitchen was Nancy's domain. She shopped, she decided if they needed new appliances or when they redecorated the kitchen. But after the divorce, Nancy didn't want to spend time in the kitchen. She would get lonely and depressed if she stayed more than five minutes there. So, she began buying microwavable dinners and instant coffee. She abandoned the breakfast nook completely, not even piling her mail there. The mail migrated to the living room coffee table. The morning paper and coffee ritual moved to the back porch or on rainy days, the living room floor. The dining room table became her home office; files, receipts, check book, and current bills laid out as a formal setting. The living room gained a new life with candles, incense, music, current novels from the library, maybe a video on Wednesday or Friday depending on what the girls from the office had planned. A warm, comfy Afghan, which her aunt gave her would be thrown on the couch, as much for the cat as for Nancy.

Dinner was much like her college days, sitting cross leg on the floor using the coffee table like a Japanese dinner table. A CD playing or maybe a game show on TV. Lunch was usually at the twenty-four-hour breakfast style restaurant next to the office building. The service was slow but adequate, the food was generally over-cooked and greasy, but it's quiet, inexpensive, and they have a smoking section. One Friday every month, generally the last or second to last Friday of the month, everybody from the office goes to lunch uptown in the historic district, where they have all the nice fancy restaurants. The service is slow and condescending, the food is under-portioned and over-seasoned, and the ambiance is pretentious and loud during lunch. And since none of her co-workers smoke, Nancy doesn't know if they have a smoking section or if those other people just wave around cigars trying to impress someone in Hollywood. Not that Nancy would want to be in a room full of cigar smokers. She just has a cigarette every once in a while, to take the edge off. She quit smoking when she graduated from college. Without the pressure of exams and research papers, she didn't crave cigarettes anymore, but during the divorce proceedings, she bought a pack and a bottle of rum. When the rum ran out she didn't buy anymore, but somehow she came home with a pack of cigarettes. And once a week it happened again.

Paul looks around the kitchen. "I can't believe I'm doing this."

"What? They want you to work a third shift?" Paul shakes his head.

"No, Joe. I can't believe that I'm scrambling eggs at a greasy truck stop."

"Look. Do what I do. Go home, clean up, get your best gal, and treat yourself to something special. Right?"

"Yeah. There's a beautiful lady I've had my eye on for a while."

"Go for it."

Nancy forgot to go shopping yesterday. The only edible things in the house were a frozen dinner and a can of tuna. Paul looks around the kitchen. Wonder why she never cooks. He gets back from shopping and cleans up while the dinner cooks. He lays out her favorite nightgown and robe, rented two classic romance movies, sets a candlelight table, and plays some classical music to accompany her dinner.

"I like this kitchen; it's airy, organized well, a few kitschy potholders and goofy refrigerator magnets, but that's nice in a way," he said.

You know a lot about a person from their kitchen. Nancy's gentle, kinda quiet, she's still trying to show control, even after the divorce, good sense of humor, she wants to live in a home not a house. And she is very attractive. That never hurts.

Paul separates the ingredients into three groups: chilled tomato soup, ground lamb kebab, and portokali ravani. Looks like she was planning on microwavable meatloaf. It's a good thing I got here when I did. Microwavable Meatloaf, truly terrifying. Someone needs to protect her. Her husband sure didn't; bastard, wracks up a bunch of bills and runs away with a younger woman.

It's in the timing. You have to figure out how long everything is going to take and then you schedule it so they are all done at once. Paul looks at the clock: 6:30. Nancy will be home in less than ten minutes, unless she makes a stop on her way home.

I could take care of Nancy, keep everything nice and neat and safe at home. Like I did for Mom after Dad died. And those assholes she went out with. If it wasn't for me, she never would have made it.

DINNER GUEST

She forgot to go shopping yesterday. But he can't bring himself to be upset about it. She has been working extra hours lately, trying to make ends meet. He's been working hard too, today is his first day off in three weeks. He cleaned the apartment, took care of the bills, which had been piling up, and was hoping to make a special dinner, but there was too much to do, and he also forgot to go shopping.

He laid out her favorite nightgown and robe, rented two romance movies, set a candlelight table, and selected some classical music to accompany dinner.

He rummaged through the refrigerator and pantry, eventually coming up with a salad, pasta, meat and sauce, and a fruit and cream dessert.

It's getting late; she'll be home soon. Too soon, dinner won't be ready, he'll still be cooking. There was too much to do and hunting for ingredients threw off his schedule.

She comes in, sees him in the kitchen, she looks around the apartment really quick. The candles are lit, the hallway light adds background illumination, her favorite aria is playing on the stereo.

"What the Hell are you doing in my house?"

"Cooking dinner."

"I can see that. I.. You.. It.. That's not what I meant."

"I'm sorry. I thought I would be done before you got home."

"Yes, that's nice, I see you've put a lot of effort into this. But.. It's.. Who are you. How did you get into my house."

"Just some guy who came in through the front door."

"Do I know you? Have we met?"

"That sounds like a pickup line."

"Yes. It does. But it isn't."

"I know. Dinner's done, why don't you sit down, and I'll serve you. After dinner you can change and watch the movies I rented."

"Thanks. Why have you done this?"

"Because I like to feel needed. Anyway, everything's set. You have a good evening. Enjoy."

"Wait. Where are you going?"

"Like I said everything's set. I can leave. I hope you have a good evening. Relax. Enjoy."

He takes off the cooking apron and picks up his jacket.

"Wait. Stay."

"I don't think that would be right. I'm a complete stranger. You don't know anything about me."

"That's fine. I'll find out. For now, I know enough. The food looks great, and I hate to eat alone."

FOR THE LOVE OF CHILI

𝕬 t the office, the workday winds down; a few of the newer people ask what and where his vacation will be. He slightly shakes and lowers his head as he tidies his desk. Someone comments that even on the day before his vacation he still doesn't loosen his tie. He's a hard worker, efficient and prepared, stays late, the Boss compliments him, he deserves his privacy. Once every year he takes a weeklong vacation. For the past 15 years he's worked for the same company; never misses work, never late. No one has found out about his vacation, no pictures, no stories, no hints. Even when he goes out with colleagues and a date, there is something held back.

When he arrives home, he washes all of his clothes, puts them neatly in the closet. He unplugs every electrical appliance, then stacks them under the hanging clothes. Only the refrigerator remains working. He empties the refrigerator of everything except 2 heads of lettuce. In the middle of the night he goes to a supermarket when there are no people around.

He buys:

2 cans of red kidney beans
1 pack of chili powder
1 bottle of cayenne pepper sauce
1 container of oregano
1 small jar of mustard
1 can of tomato paste
1 container of black pepper
1 container of white pepper
1 container of salt
1 block of Colby cheese
1 pound of fresh ground steak
3 eggs
1 loaf of natural whole wheat bread

3 medium Vidalia onions
4 cloves of garlic
1 pack of non-filter cigarettes
3 bottles of 1973 California white wine
1 bottle of 8-year-old sour mash whiskey
and for this year's change:
1 container of peanut oil

He pays with 2 dollar bills.

When he gets home, he puts all the food away. He locks all the doors and windows. Draws down blinds and curtains. He pushes all the furniture up against the doors and walls. The dresser's drawers facing the wall. He drapes red velvet over all the furniture, placing and lighting yellow candles around the room. He strips. He puts his suit into the hamper. He unpacks the white silk suit from the dry-cleaning bags. He hangs it in the kitchen. He bathes: 1/2 cup mineral oil, water, burns frankincense incense, and scrubs down with a loofa. He dries and wraps himself in a black cotton robe.

He lies down in the middle of the room. For the next 2 days he eats only lettuce and drinks water.

On day 3 he sings old delta blues songs to himself-- he changes into the white silk suit. He brings out his special cooking utensils.

He puts the beans in a pot with 1/2 cup of water. He adds-- 1/2 teaspoon of chili powder; 2/3 teaspoon cayenne pepper sauce; 1 1/4 teaspoon oregano; 1 1/2 tablespoon tomato paste; 1 tablespoon mustard; 1/2 teaspoon salt; 1 teaspoon white pepper. He turns the burner to simmer, he places the lid on the pot.

He toasts 5 slices whole wheat bread, cuts off and eats the crusts, crumbles it. mixing in 1/4 teaspoon salt; 1/4 teaspoon black pepper; 1/2 teaspoon oregano, all in a clear glass bowl.

He peels 2 cloves of garlic, thinly slicing 1 and dicing the other. He pours 1/4 cup white wine into a skillet, he scatters the garlic slices in the wine, then scatters the diced garlic over it all. He sautés it for 3 minutes. He drains the wine and separates the garlic into 2 piles, more or less equal.

He peels and dices the onions, placing 2 into the skillet with 1/4 cup peanut oil. He sautés them until they are golden brown. He drains the oil and places the sautéed onions in a pile near the garlic.

He peels the last 2 cloves of garlic-- slicing 1 and dicing 2. He places them with the un-cooked diced onion.

He separates 2 eggs, adding the white to the breadcrumbs and the entire other egg. He adds-- the ground steak; 1/4 teaspoon cayenne pepper sauce; 1/4 teaspoon mustard; the sautéed onions; 1 pile sautéed garlic; and 2 shots whiskey. He reaches into the bowl vigorously kneading the mixture until it is thoroughly mixed.

He flattens the meat into a skillet and puts the other pile of sautéed garlic into the beans, which he stirs 5 times. He puts the burner for the meat on medium high. He lights a cigarette. When he is done smoking, he flips over all the meat, breaking it into small chunks. He then lights another cigarette, smokes it, takes the meat off the stove and drains the juices.

He takes the cheese and slices it into small slivers 1/2 inch long. He places the cheese next to the cut onions and garlic.

He places the meat in with the beans, turning the burner up to medium. He stirs the mixture together, drinks 1 shot whiskey and smokes 1 cigarette.

He uncorks the chilled wine and places it in the middle of the floor letting it breathe.

He turns the burner back down to simmer, stirs the chili, then scoops out 1 bowl full. He grabs 1/2 handful of cut onion, garlic, and cheese and places that on top of the chili in the bowl.

He sits down next to the wine and eats until the whole bowl of chili is gone. It takes him 23 hours, with many breaks. He finishes the last swig of wine.

He smiles. He belches. It is done. 1 of these years he won't uncover the furniture, he won't plug in the appliances back in, he won't go back to work; he lies down. Some people have dreams bigger than imagination itself. Next year he'll add rice.

He sleeps a while, when he wakes he begins unwrapping the furniture, moving everything back in place.

ARTHUR, A FRAGMENT

e hears the footfalls behind him. Then the click of a pistol being cocked - too close to his head to miss.

"You know what I want."

"I don't got anything. " Arthur stalls.

"Come on, give it to me."

"Look, I don't have any money nor any drugs. If you shoot me, the only thing you'll have is one less bullet." And my corpse, Arthur thinks.

"I.. I don't want drugs, just give me your money."

"If this is your first mugging, you've got the wrong person, since this isn't for drugs. I hope it's worth it."

"Don't FUCK WITH ME, MAN!"

Arthur makes a fist: spins; his left arm as a block; fist follows. A split in the universe; his stomach; through which all the hordes of Hell shout "BANG!" He drops to his knees, pooling on himself. Focusing, he sees his assailant. A boy lying flat out, bleeding from the nose. I'm twice his size and at least ten years older. Little David as always slays Goliath. Then the world is dark.

Murmurings, the wailing of a cat, hypnotic blinking -red, blue, blue, red. Nothing. Voices. Nothing.

White man in white uniform: "Damn, idiots shooting each other..."

Nothing. Jolt of pain, movement. Jungle. Medic, Medic, we've wounded. Incoming Charlie. Sergeant, have your men clear the LZ.

Arthur wakes to the modern plastic pleasure of two tubes shoved so far down his nose, he can feel them in his throat. A headache, something plastic stuck to the left side of his head.

He opens his eyes, painful white blinding light. Plastic fluid filled tubes jutting in and out of his arms, less irksome than those in his nose, show his gains and losses, drop by drop. Chest and stomach held together with tape and glue, sharp seams of pain. Nothing.

"So, you're awake now. Glad to see it. Can't sleep away your entire life, now, can you?" She smiles, a trained and institutionalized friendliness.

"Where's David? I mean, the boy who shot me?" He bleats in goatlike hoarseness, seeing Loki approaching.

"Sorry, I only know you." Beautifully, mechanically said.

"Water?"

"I'll see what I can do."

Arthur thinks back:

"Sorry that I dropped this on ya so sudden - Art, but I just talked to my accountant today, and that bank guy gonna auction the place. It's the only way I ain't gonna be hitting the street. Maybe the new owner will hire ya back. You bring good customers. But don't'chu worry none. I'll mail ya your check first thing."

Right. And now a hospital bill and no insurance.

The nurse reenters the partitioned room: "Mr. Abraham, here's your water. If that'll be all? Just buzz me if you need anything."

"At home was little left, and none abroad; there was no anchor, none, to hold by,' Oh well, Tennyson. This Arthur isn't dead yet."

Arthur closes his eyes, thanks his high school English teacher, and...

Nothingness.

CONTROL OF THE SITUATION

ouise checked the clock again. It had been fifteen minutes since she last checked. Rob was now an hour and fifteen minutes late. He said he would pick her up at 7:30 PM. It was getting to be too late for dinner. Her stomach ached. She had only eaten a light lunch. It was a busy day at work and her boss had surprised her with extra tasks. It was someone else's job; Anne's job, actually.

Anne had neglected to do the work having overbooked herself in pointless but noticeable meetings. She knew how to play office politics. She held big meetings to discuss ideas that the upper management loved to talk about but did nothing to implement. The managers all saw her at these meetings and they thought of her as an idea person. What she really did was to reiterate what they had said earlier as if she too had come to the same conclusions. She then complimented them on their great insights and understanding. They ate it up. But the day-to-day work of keeping the company running had to fall upon someone's desk, and that is where Louise was noticed. She plowed through work and avoided most meetings. And frequently only ate half of her lunch at her desk in order to keep up the demands of her job and Anne's slack.

Anne would complement Louise: 'She is a hard worker. Not an innovator, though. She's so nice. It would be nicer if she could see the big picture and not always get caught up in the weeds.' Another fifteen minutes went by. Louise chuckled at how consistent she was being in checking the time: the world's slowest metronome. Rob hadn't responded to the text she sent forty-five minutes ago. She didn't want to seem desperate or clingy, so she didn't send any other texts after that. Since she was hungry and dressed up, she decided to go to the sports bar down the street. It was her usual hang out and she knew the staff and some of the other regulars. She could get some bar food and still not feel quite alone, even if she was.

Rob and Anne were sitting in a booth at the bar. Louise slipped back out the door, hoping no one noticed her. She turned around and bumped into her usual waitress, Amy, coming back from a smoke break.

"Hey. Are you leaving already? I didn't even know you were here tonight?"

"Uhm, yeah. I couldn't stay long. I gotta go."

"Hold up. You couldn't have been here for more than five minutes. I just stepped out. What's going on?"

"Nothing. I just don't feel well. I should probably go home."

Rob had noticed her by then. He waved. He wasn't exactly smiling, teeth were showing, but there was no happiness in his face. Anne turned to face Louise in the doorway, she too had no joy in her toothy expression.

Louise strained a smile back at them and slightly waved. She turned back to Amy and let her face sadden.

"Rob and I had a date tonight. He blew me off."

"Oh, honey, I'm so sorry. I didn't know."

"Too late now." Louise walked to their booth. Anne slid over, giving enough room for Louise to sit down and join them.

"You look nice," Anne said. "You changed out of your frumpy work clothes."

"Yeah, I guess," Louise answered.

"Have a big night planned?" Anne asked.

"Not really. Just thought I would come out for a little bit." Louise checked the clock, half an hour since she last looked.

"Funny, I ran into Anne here tonight and we ended up talking. It turns out we both know you. Who would have guessed? Small world and all." Rob said.

"I suppose. This is close to my apartment. And not too far from the office," said Louise.

Amy came to the table, bringing Louise a glass of chardonnay.

"This is from Mike. The nice man at the bar," Amy smiled. "I can vouch for him. He's a sweetheart. Why don't you go say hi to him?" Amy nodded to Louise.

Louise smiled, genuinely. She turned and looked at Rob and Anne. "It would be rude if I didn't at least thank him. You two have a good night. Nice seeing you both." She got up and went over to Mike.

"Hi. Thank you for the drink."

"You're welcome," Mike said. "I've seen you here before and Amy told me that guy was gaslighting you. So we thought I could rescue you. I'm not going to try anything. I'm happily married and my wife works nights so I come here. Are you OK?"

"I'm better now. Thanks."

TWINS

Janey pulls her light-blue sports-coupe into the parking lot, she's twenty minutes earlier than necessary, she doesn't like to be caught in the rush. All those other cars in her way; screaming, silly girls, chit-chatting, giggly, huddled in small clusters, meandering toward the conglomeration of mothers in idling automobiles. Blocking her in and holding her up, as if she didn't work, like those other women, as if her husband (whom is still her first and only) didn't expect a clean, respectable home, with a good meal waiting (none of that communistic fast-food in this house).

Janey takes the brief opportunity to look into her rear-view mirror (angled just right, so that she doesn't have to adjust it, to confirm her make-up's integrity). It is important to maintain oneself, her m other (God-rest-her-soul) was always picture perfect at all times, she taught Janey all the keys to being a real woman, including the ever-special ability of how to cook without the use of those horridly tacky aprons (only servants and the awkward wear those garments). Janey is impeccable, that's why she's early, and has idled her car right in front of the parking lot exit. Some people have complained about this, using the red herring of her blocking the parking lot exit to mask their true jealousy and lack of class and upbringing. After all, Janey's husband is a wealthy doctor, there's nothing wrong with being a mortician - people always die.

Janey's beautiful girls are worth the additional time out of her schedule, even though they are at that icky awkward age, and not yet at a stage where they will gracefully float from room to room. Janey has the firmest of motherly belief in them and their potential to become wondrous, graceful wives of doctors, as is tradition for women in their family; lawyers have become acceptable, take Cousin Ruthie, for example. Janey was so proud to have had twins, even though it took her nine years, it finally came true, her duty of being the first woman in her family to have twins (as her Grand-Mother [god-rest-her-soul] had told her she would, when she was ten). Now the only obligations she has left, are to bury her husband, and see her twin daughters married off in a simultaneous wedding. If only they would learn how not to sweat, it's so embarrassing.

TWINS TWO

Melissa gets up from her desk and walks to her locker, where she'll wait for Clarissa to meet her. She watches the other girls as they start congregating in the halls, talking about how mean their teachers are, and boys, and television, and boys on television. Melissa tries to eaves-drop on the other girls, as she always does when they talk about boys, going to an all-girls school, the only boys she knows are the ones on television, but not the ones the other girls talk about, because her Mother doesn't let her watch those shows, because they are morally corrupt and present a picture of the world devoid of grace and decorum.

Clarissa skips up to Melissa and tugs at the edges of her sister's long blonde hair. Melissa shakes her head forcefully, then pats her sister's brown halo of hair. They hold hands and walk out to their mother's car. There is a line of six other cars behind her, honking and saying words that Melissa recognizes as dirty words, which she overheard in the gym locker room and the bathroom. She cannot let her mother know that she even recognizes them as English (even though the definitions still elude her). Melissa puts Clarissa into the child-seat in the back of the car, straightens Clarissa's flower-print dress and pulls up her white socks.

Melissa gets into the front seat, gives her mother a gingerly peck on the cheek, and buckles her seat belt. Janey leans over and straightens Melissa's flower-print dress and pulls up her white socks. Melissa is admonished for having scuffed shoes, as the other parents beep their horns and gain in volume in their dirty talk.

REHEATED COFFEE

℃ o: JimBloom
From: EZ#
Subject: blog & enumeration
TEXT:
the economics of the situation
Ad revenue w/   eyes on the page &&   click thru
enuf ppl
like java & yr pour
4 a cheque paid 2 U
I (e)-Deposited it in
crypo-currency
to avoid libtard taxes
& bypass deep-state monitoring
(.)^(.)
LOOKING 4wd 2
yr next Blog (keep writing):

yrs,
EZ#

***

In previous writings on the coffee blog, I have reviewed coffee
shops throughout the city. I discussed the various types of beans
and how to process them for preparing the best cup. I have gone
into detail about extreme methods of gaining flavor, including the
cerval cat poop coffee technique. I touched on coffee alternatives
such as kava, cacao, yerba mate, and chicory. I even presented an
overview of teas. I explored the historical traditions of coffee's
impact on different cultures. I talked about how coffee integrated
into the lifestyle of the United States of America. In today's blog, I
will look into the representations of coffee in popular music.
The most popular theme of coffee songs is having a hangover. The
folk saying that coffee cures a hangover is played out where the
singer who is hungover reminisces about their current situation.
The most frequent cause of the drinking binge is a heartbreak.

The next most popular theme represented in coffee songs is that of a new romance. Typically, in these songs a couple will be drinking coffee together. Sometimes they are out on a date, but other instances the drinking of coffee represents an early morning where they have spent the night together.

The rest of the coffee songs cover the emotions and actions of reflection, regret, planning, and nostalgia. Coffee and the songs about coffee are the times to sit and think about one's state in the world. The singer and listener think about what went right and wrong and then ponder what could have been.

I have come to the conclusion that songs about coffee are the arc of the life cycle of relationships. Coffee is the unifying flow throughout the phases of romance. As I have been saying in this blog for years, love of coffee is that coffee is love.

Follow my Coffee Blog for all the best Java pondering.

***

Jim's dreams faded from his memory as he fumbled with the snooze of his alarm clock, the epic adventures and mythological entities receded to his subconsciousness. Finally, having conquered the technology, he got out of bed and took a shower – shampoo in his eyes, cyclopean fumbling, a careful shave, the tired beginnings of daily planning; picking the right outfit for the day (guessing at how the day will go) and looking the right part for what is expected. Making dark roast Kona Hawaiian coffee for watching the news and checking emails – time drifts quickly as attention wanders, a poured cup of coffee is left on the counter, Jim rushes to the subway, mind racing and barely on schedule.

Wind and sleet accompany Jim the three blocks to the subway entrance. Jostled and slipping in dark puddles down the stairs, he quickly descends to the platform. With only one place to stand, the train bounces sore hips and misaligned back, Jim crosses the river. Paramedics block off the station, trying to resuscitate a heart-attack;

life or death, the crowd pushes around in inconvenience, in a shadowed corner Charon waits. Jim finds a way down to his connecting train with the comfort of a cold, hard plastic seat.

Wind and sleet greet Jim as he goes to the independently owned and operated coffee shop, for muffin and a cup (medium-dark roast, Liberica bean with a dollop of whipped cream). Favorite barista has Jim's order waiting behind the counter.

"Sorry, running late" in not a carbon-copy chain store where standardization and uniformity are the means of existence and production nor a set from F*R*I*E*N*D*S pretending to be more than a pretentious coffee shop, but an actual place where people enjoyed coffee and all the other trappings were there only to enhance the coffee experience.

There is the office, coworkers, hierarchical superiors, indecipherable metrics on the belief of productivity, attempts at efficiency (without appearing lazy), aimless daydreaming, unproductive meetings, take-out lunch at his desk, unread emails, disjointed phone calls, unexpected changes to projects, and the torturous vending machine coffee.

Train ride through tunnels and across bridges to the borough for an optometrist. The guardian greeter dispassionately assigns a waiting station which Jim acquiesces. Time drifts slowly, a crowd dissipates slowly, one vanishing after another into the cavernous maw. Jim asks how he was lost when others had passed along as he loomed in the room.

– "What is your name again?"

– "There is no record of you. Nobody."

– "Your file was misplaced, please, go in now."

Machines, lights, tests, chemicals, to reach a blurry disoriented dilation – diagnosis and prescription. Squinting, street level, fumbling with mobile phone to reach a Gypsy cab, avoiding the ride apps, preferring the traditional side gig hustler, fighting against the taxi authority, a strange person in a car, willing to go in a direction for a price. Jim's vision rendered him unable to navigate, a ship cursed by Poseidon and tossed around by a kraken, lost in the sea, he had a direction to wander, but no other means of arriving.

The illegal and subversive driver maneuvered the vehicle through the mazes of the city streets playing carefully with the legality of right turns on red, speed limits, and yellow light timings – NASCAR jockeying for pack position. A traffic jam backed up two lanes yet not the third, a side streetcar darts across.

T-boned sedan.

– "This is why I don't let them through, they can't see that last lane – like being torpedoed by a U-Boat."

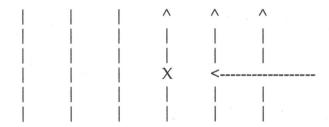

I Ching hexagram = conflict or arguing or predicted lawsuit: lower with water and outer with force. The character, Jī: to hit, to break. Traffic diagram.

The illegal and subversive driver maneuvered the vehicle through the mazes of the city streets playing carefully with safety – bootlegger avoiding detection.

Mulligan's Tavern was thronged and cacophonous. Nora sipped her espresso martini as Jim approached the table so she wouldn't feel obligated to be the first person to acknowledge his presence. EZ# grabbed a chair from another table to make welcoming intrusiveness for Jim. G was telling the same story about the rose buttons. (Alice would interrupt G and add story points.)

The waiter transported the Irish coffee. Jim sipped it.
EZ# and Thom debated bitcoin, the Euro, and how to monetize their podcasts.

[insert: blah blah, blah].

Ernie dropped by the table for a quick 'Hello, there!' Somehow argued with G which EZ# had to break up. Went off to another bar by himself did Ernie. Alice was tired, had work on Saturday so she and G went home. Thom called the evening quits and EZ# went for karaoke. Waiter delivered another; Jim ingested as did Nora. The bar quieted and eventually the lights flickered.

Wind and sleet escort Jim and Nora between Gypsy cab and door. Warm sheets, warm bodies.

Morning:

Nora sees the left-over coffee on the counter, microwaves it, and sits on the couch.

***
"Reheated Coffee" Spotify playlist:
https://open.spotify.com/playlist/5quh0ttGez8kSZcYegW1HD?si=240b1e e78fd44d28
#

ACKNOWLEDGMENTS

I gratefully thank Karen Cline-Tardiff for believing in my work and encouraging this book to come together. Brooke Feichtl has been an insightful and helpful editor. Andrew Hilliard was a great collaborator in the cover design. I appreciate everyone at Gnashing Teeth Publishing for ushering this book into existence.

I humbly thank Lesli Richardson, Jeff Morris, Richard Lee Byers, and Craig Spector for their support of my writing.

"Autobiography" was first published in *experimental-experimental-literature*, 2019

"The Best Little Zombie House in Florida" was first published in *Cliterature Journal* (Appetite), 2010

"ThE BugMAn" was first published in *Brave New Word* #14.5, 2019

"Chicken's Foot" was first published in *Cliterature Journal* (Hags & Witches), 2007

"Control of the Situation" was first published in *Door is a Jar* #13, 2020

"Dinner Guest" was first published in *Cliterature Journal* (Appetite), 2010

"For the Love of Chili" was first published in *Heat the Grease, We're Frying Up Some Poetry*, edited by Karen Cline-Tardiff (Gnashing Teeth Publishing) 2019

"Housewife" was first published in *The Alien Buddha's House of Horrors* #3, edited by Red Focks (Alien Buddha Press) 2020

"Savages" was first published in *Cliterature Journal* (The Jungle), 2009

"Selected Writings of Ignoscire the Etruscan" was first published in *Flammable Art: Works on Paper at the Image Brewery Gallery,* curated by Bob Dorsey 1997

"Sinbad's Account of the Island of Wood People and Fire" was first published in *Sinbad and the Winds of Destiny: The First Six Voyages and More,* edited by Kevin Candela (KHP Kent Hill Publishing) 2016

ABOUT THE AUTHOR

Yrik-Max Valentonis's books *Cranium Theatre* and *120 Days of Gomorrah* are available from Alien Buddha Press. His comics and writings have appeared in the chapbooks: *iDEAL* and *this is visual poetry*; the anthologies: *Alien Buddha's Block Party, Alien Buddha's House of Horrors 3, Animal Blessings, Divided Again, Heat the Grease We're Frying Up Some Poetry, Sinbad and the Winds of Destiny,* and *Zombie Nation: St. Pete.* He earned a BA in English and American Literature from the University of South Florida and a MFA in Poetry & Prose from Naropa University.

Yrik-Max Valentonis wanders through the urban landscape seeking out fairy circles. He makes puppets so other people can see his imaginary friends. He steals apples to justify his philosophy. He is Baba Yaga's favorite grandson. A friend of the Fey. A journeyer to the Realms. A teller of tales. A collector of Gargoyles.

Milton Keynes UK
Ingram Content Group UK Ltd.
UKHW041826070624
443834UK00003B/49

A collection of quaint and quirky speculative fictions, Y.M. Valentonis' *Short Stories Without Provocation* are experimental narratives from the beginnings of history to today's coffee blog post. These cozy-horror, bizarro-folklore, and slipstream tales have a Southern Acid Gothic flare. The eight sections are thematic patchwork storiy composites expanding upon each other.

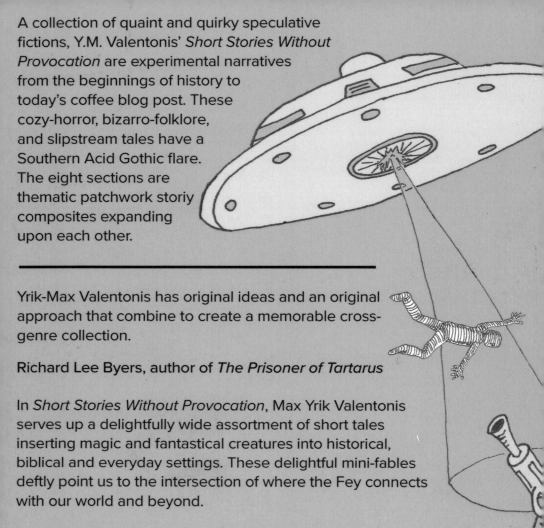

Yrik-Max Valentonis has original ideas and an original approach that combine to create a memorable cross-genre collection.

Richard Lee Byers, author of *The Prisoner of Tartarus*

In *Short Stories Without Provocation*, Max Yrik Valentonis serves up a delightfully wide assortment of short tales inserting magic and fantastical creatures into historical, biblical and everyday settings. These delightful mini-fables deftly point us to the intersection of where the Fey connects with our world and beyond.

R.W. Marcus, Author of the *Tales of the Annigan Cycle* Series

Surrealistic mental nut-punches, with a heaping dash of bizarro strong-arming magical realism into crying "uncle." Dipping into this collection is a mental melange that is best enjoyed by just sitting back and letting it happen (in the best way possible). Tasty snacks and teasing tidbits that soon have you wondering how you got here and leave you wanting more. Buckle up, buttercup--it's a bumpy ride. And those are the best kind.

USA Today Bestselling Author Tymber Dalton

GNASHING TEETH PUBLISHING

ISBN 979-8-9898345-3-2

9 798989 834532